Published by Higher Bank Books

FIGHT FOR DARKNESS

A Post Apocalyptic EMP Survival Thriller

RYAN CASEY

GET A POST APOCALYPTIC NOVEL FOR FREE

To instantly receive an exclusive post apocalyptic novel totally free, sign up for Ryan Casey's author newsletter at: ryancaseybooks.com/fanclub

CHAPTER ONE

Aoife saw the dead children lying frozen inside the tent and felt a familiar twinge of sadness.

It was freezing. Bitter cold. So cold she could barely feel her lips, or her entire face for that matter. She'd seen the camp from quite a way away. A few tents in an open area of the woods. The remains of a fire, which looked like it'd burned out long ago. Snow falling heavily, completely covering the three tents.

And the moment Aoife saw the tents, she knew what she was going to find. The red flags were there from the off. The old firewood, which must've been lit yonks ago. The way the snow covered the tents like a blanket.

Sure signs that this camp was abandoned.

And yet...

Something made Aoife walk up to it.

Hope? She wasn't sure. Hadn't felt any real hope in a long, long time.

Hope was useless. Hope was fucking dangerous.

But whatever it was, something drew her to the tents.

There was nobody inside the first one. A few scraps of frozen rotten meat, which mice scurried around. Nasty smell in there, like something dead. At one point, the smell might've made her heave. But she was used to the stench of death now.

She moved on to the second tent and found the children.

A boy and a girl. Couldn't be older than ten. Icy film over their bodies. Their skin looked grey, lifeless. Both of them curled up together, frozen solid.

That twinge of sadness, then. A million stories racing through her mind. The thought of these poor souls dying in the cold. The thought of them seeing each other and knowing embracing was the only way to stay warm.

She looked at them and let the sadness in fully.

Then she took a deep breath and let it go.

She searched the tent for anything useful. Any supplies that would help. The best thing she could find was an insulated blanket. That could come in handy. Any extra layer of warmth came in handy in this bitter, freezing winter.

She climbed over the frozen children to grab it when she noticed something.

A mark. A bloody mark on the neck of the little blonde girl.

A stab wound.

Aoife's stomach sank. She thought they'd frozen to death at first, but this made more sense. Someone had killed the girl. Did the boy have a similar mark? She couldn't see one.

What did it matter anyway? A tragedy was a tragedy.

She climbed over the kids and grabbed the blanket. Went to leave the tent. A part of her imagined she was going to find someone outside waiting for her. Someone familiar. Max. Or Kayleigh. Or Rex. And for a moment, it comforted her. For a moment, it made her feel slightly less... well, *alone*.

But her stomach turned the more she thought of all of them.

Her jaw tensed up.

The gunshot.

The shouts.

The darkness.

Best not to think about what happened.

Not today.

She was going to go back to Kayleigh and Rex, and everything was going to be okay.

She turned around when she got to the tent door. Looked back over at the kids.

Whatever happened here, she just hoped they hadn't suffered too much.

She took a deep breath of the bitterly cold air and stepped back out into the deep, crunchy snow.

She looked around at the scene. The snow was thick as hell here, right up to her knees. It hadn't stopped snowing for God knows how long. Felt like it'd been snowing for about six months. She didn't really know what date it was anymore. Lost track. She didn't know whether Christmas had passed yet. Didn't know whether she'd missed the four-year anniversary of the blackout. She didn't even know if she'd missed her birthday.

What did it matter?

Those dates were useful milestones and markers in the old world.

But all that mattered in this world was survival.

She looked at the trees, draped in snow. The grey skies above. She looked around at these woods and breathed in that freezing air. Sometimes, she liked to imagine she was young again. That she was a kid, here with her dad, a sense of mystery and adventure about trips like this.

Imagining she was young again, imagining the way she used to feel... it was the only way she could remind herself of those feelings.

Happiness.

Joy.

Even sadness.

Those emotions were in short supply now.

Any emotions were in short supply now.

She looked around at that third and final tent, and something inside told her not to go over to it. To stay away from it. That something was hiding in there that she didn't want to find.

But curiosity got the better of her. Naturally, really. She didn't exactly live the most interesting or stimulating life anymore. It didn't take much to capture her curiosity.

She looked over at that red tent. The front of it zipped up. The material swaying in the breeze.

Stay away, Aoife. Stay well away...

But she couldn't help herself.

She walked over to it.

Footsteps crunching through the thick snow.

The icy wind pounding against her. So noisy she couldn't hear anything other than herself.

She stood outside that tent.

Knife in hand.

And then she yanked the zip up.

The tent was empty.

Completely empty.

She gulped. Took a deeper breath.

All in your head. There's nothing here. Just get out of here. Just go.

She turned around to walk away when she saw a man standing in front of her.

He had nasty sore bald patches on his head, which extended to his face, an angry shade of red. He had a long black beard. He was painfully thin.

And he was holding on to a dead squirrel. A dead squirrel that it looked like he'd taken a bite out of.

She could see the madness in his eyes. She knew what it looked like. She'd seen enough crazies to know one.

She lifted her knife. Mostly just to show him she wasn't messing if he came at her.

He stared at her with that blank, wide-eyed stare.

Don't do a thing. Don't you fucking dare make a move.

And then, out of nowhere, he spoke.

"For my kids," he said. "They—they—they need their br breakfast. Please. Don't—don't hurt me. I'm just—I'm just feedin' my kids. Please."

She saw the man begging, pleading. Saw the tears in those glazed eyes. And she lowered her knife. A fresh wave of sympathy crashing over her.

He was just a dad.

Just a dad trying to feed his kids.

His kids who were already gone.

And looking into those bloodshot eyes... Aoife knew this man already knew the fate of his children. He knew this was all an illusion. He knew this was a lie he told himself to make himself feel better.

The power lies could have to create a sense of comfort. A sense of reassurance.

She watched him walk towards the tent the kids were inside. Watched him step into it. Heard him talking.

"Hello, my little ones. I've got your—your favourite. Squirrel. Yes. That's right. I will. I will..."

"That's sad," a voice said, right beside Aoife.

She looked around. Saw Kayleigh standing there. Looking younger now, somehow. Blonder. Fresher faced. Rex panting beside her.

Aoife nodded. Looked back at the tents. "Yeah. Yeah, it is."

She thought about the gunshot.

Thought about Yuri standing opposite, gun to Kayleigh's head.

She thought about all of it, and then she pushed it away, all to one side.

You don't have to think about that now.

And then, with her two friends—her *only* friends—she walked away.

CHAPTER TWO

"You really need to find yourself a new friend or something."

Aoife felt the hairs on the back of her neck stand on end the second she heard Kayleigh speak. She was always so critical these days. She never seemed to have anything nice to say. Not since the day everything changed, eighteen months ago.

Not since Aoife held that pistol. Pointed it at the power source while Yuri stood opposite, gun to Kayleigh's head.

Not since Aoife pulled that trigger...

But then could Aoife blame her, really?

She couldn't imagine she'd have much nice to say to Kayleigh if the roles had been reversed.

She looked down at the fire before her. Listened to the wood crackling away. Smelled the smoke. Something was comforting about that sound and those smells. Even if the warmth of the fire was doing absolutely nothing to cut through just how fucking freezing Aoife was.

She lived a life of constant shivering. Of numb fingertips and frostbitten ears.

But it was just the life she lived.

It was the world she lived in now.

"Your punishment, you could say."

Aoife gritted her teeth when she heard Kayleigh speak. She closed her eyes. Tried to focus on that crackling wood. Tried to absorb any little bit of warmth from it that she could.

Tried everything to avoid hearing what Kayleigh was saying.

But she carried on. Incessantly.

"After everything that happened, it's probably the least you deserve."

"Shut up," Aoife said.

"What was that?"

"I said, shut up!"

Her voice echoed through the woods. The flames flickered. She heard Rex whine somewhere just out of sight as she stood there, fists clenched.

"I'm just saying," Kayleigh said. Smug look on her face. Knowing full well she'd hit a nerve. "Actions have consequences."

"I know that," Aoife said, sitting back down, holding her hands out in front of the fire. "I know that all too well. And I don't need reminding all the time. Especially not by you."

She looked into the flames. It was getting dark. She'd have to move on from here soon. She didn't want to run into anyone. The people who were left weren't the kind anyone wanted to bump into. There weren't many people out here, for one. And those who were... generally, they weren't exactly good eggs anymore.

She knew fire drew attention. She had to warm up. She'd have to skip a meal today.

And then she'd have to go find somewhere to rest.

Another day in the life of a survivor.

"You should think about it, though," Kayleigh said.

Aoife felt that stabbing pain of irritation once more. She just wanted Kayleigh to shut the fuck up. "Think about what?"

"Finding new friends. I mean, it's lonely out here for us three. If we find someone new, at least we might be able to start again. And they never have to know what you did. Or who you are."

The way she said those words, so bitter, so cold. Colder than the air itself. It made Aoife wonder if Kayleigh was even on her side at all. If she was even her friend anymore.

But then she already knew the answer to that question, didn't she?

She saw the look in Rex's eyes, too. The way the fire danced in his pupils. The way he stared at her. Like even *he* knew.

And like he judged her for it.

"I don't need friends."

"Everyone needs friends," Kayleigh said.

"Friends are a burden."

"You're sounding like your old self. Not wanting to connect through fear. Not wanting to get close to anyone in case you lose them..."

"That's not what it is," Aoife said.

And she was telling the truth. It was different now. She used to have that fear of connecting with others in case she lost them or in case she was responsible for their deaths. But things were different now.

She didn't want friends because they were a burden.

She didn't want responsibilities because they weighed her down.

She just wanted to keep on surviving, keep on living like this, going about things her own way.

She was... well, not *happy* this way.

But it served her well.

"You're probably right," Kayleigh said. "But sometimes I wonder if you're just trying to convince yourself. After what happened."

The second she said those words, the images filled her mind again.

Yuri.

The gun to Kayleigh's head.

Aoife pulling the trigger.

Running.

Running to get away and...

"We don't have to think about that," Kayleigh said. "Not today."

Aoife's shoulders softened. Her whole body relaxed in an instant. She was glad Kayleigh said that. Glad she'd put a line under it for the day. She wasn't always so forgiving.

Today wasn't nice as it was. The frozen kids. The grieving father, still trying to feed them.

That was enough bullshit to deal with for one day.

She held her hands in front of the fire until it fizzled out. Heard animals howling in the darkness. Wild dogs. Probably a few animals escaped from zoos, too. She'd heard whispers of bears and tigers. Lucky enough not to run into one yet. Hell, maybe it'd make for a bit of excitement in her life.

She looked up at the darkness, up at the stars, and wondered where the next day would take her.

"If you could go back," Kayleigh said. "Back to before all this. Do you think you'd live life any differently?"

Aoife thought of her life before.

A life of trying to get into uni to study that zoology degree.

A life that had so much potential but so much pain.

And then she thought of the life she'd lived since and how much she barely recognised herself anymore.

"I think we'd all do things differently," she said. "Now come on. We'd better find some place to rest."

She covered the remainder of the fire with the snow.

She looked over at Kayleigh, at Rex, just for a second.

"I'm sorry," she whispered under her breath. "I... I'm sorry."

Kayleigh and Rex were completely enshrouded by the darkness.

She closed her eyes. Turned away from them.

"I wish I could've done things differently."

Then, she swallowed a lump in her throat, and she walked.

CHAPTER THREE

She was in the middle of the power source again.

She had no idea how this was possible. But it was. She was standing here, pistol in hand. Pointing it right at the source of all electricity to Sanctuary. Shaking. Heart beating so fast it felt like it might break through her ribcage, explode in a bloody mess.

All around her, the torchlights of Yuri's people as they looked down at her. That nervous look in Yuri's eyes as he held the gun to Kayleigh's head.

"Don't," he said. "You don't want to do this, Aoife. You don't want to destroy power for everyone. You don't want to destroy hope for everyone."

But Aoife knew how this went already.

She knew exactly what happened next.

There was nothing she could do to stop herself. The fate of this entire standoff had already been decided. It had already been written, long ago.

"Aoife," Yuri said.

She looked right into Kayleigh's eyes, now. And as she looked into them at the time, she was convinced Kayleigh was nodding her head. Urging her on. Encouraging her to do what they both knew was right. Because Yuri couldn't be in control of this electricity. He was too powerful with it. And his intentions weren't good.

She had to do this for the good of humanity itself.

But now, did she see something different?

Did she see Kayleigh crying?

Was she *shaking* her head?

She wanted to stop. Didn't want to pull the trigger. She wanted to know if there was another option. Another way.

She wanted to stop herself.

"Aoife," Yuri said. "Don't..."

But then she felt herself saying the words.

Saying them just as she'd said them on that day.

"There's one thing more important than power."

"And what's that?" Yuri asked.

"Connection," Aoife said.

And then she pulled the trigger and...

Her eyes opened.

She jolted upright. Gasping for breath. Sweating like mad, even though it was bitter cold.

She looked around the room she was in. Dark. Moonlight shining through the windows. *It's okay. You're okay. You're safe. Everything is going to be okay.*

She took a few deep breaths in, felt her belly rise, then descend again. Did this a few more times until she felt a bit calmer. It was then that the shivering restarted. The freezing cold. Her fingernails were blue like they'd been painted. She couldn't feel her toes.

"It's alright, Rex. We're... we're gonna be okay."

She heard Rex snoring away. At least he was comfortable.

She looked around this room. Top floor of a semi-detached house just outside the woods. She'd stayed here before. Pretty run down and not in the best condition. Bird shit and feathers everywhere. Looked like a pigeon had got in here a while ago. Judging by the smell of things, it'd died in here too.

But it was one of the warmer places around here.

And besides. What else did she have, really?

Where else was there to go?

She didn't have any direction in mind. There *was* no direction to head towards.

And sure. She knew about the other districts. The other places like Sanctuary. Supposed safe-havens.

But she wasn't going there.

She was done with those places. She couldn't go there after what'd happened at Sanctuary. She couldn't live with herself knowing…

No.

Kayleigh was right.

Didn't have to go down that road today.

She looked around the room. Kayleigh wasn't here now. That was a good thing. Must've gone out. She didn't sleep much. When she did, she slept funny hours and preferred to sleep on her own.

Aoife was grateful for the peace. She didn't get much peace from Kayleigh these days.

She leaned back against the pillow and felt Rex's warmth by her side. It wasn't enough to take the icy coldness away, but it was something.

It made her feel happy.

It made her feel less… alone.

She lay there a while until she realised she wasn't going to get any more sleep. So she got up. Walked around this room. Walked over to the window, looked outside, out at the streets. At the moon. She'd read something before the blackout. If you can't sleep, get up, do something productive.

And right now, as unappealing as the cold felt… it was rare she got a moment away from Kayleigh.

She was going to go out, and she was going to take a walk.

Fuck. She was cold as it was. Wouldn't make much different in the scheme of things, would it?

She walked down the creaky stairs, being careful to stay quiet. If Kayleigh was sleeping, and she heard her, she'd wake and join her. She didn't want that. Wanted her own space to think. Or rather, to *not* think. To just be at peace.

She reached the front door and heard the floorboards behind her creak.

Her stomach sank. Her body froze. Kayleigh. She was awake, and she was going to follow her.

She opened the front door and closed it as quickly and quietly as she could. Rex was inside, staring through the bedroom windows at her, wagging his docked tail. He was okay in there. Kayleigh had a mean streak, but she wouldn't do anything to hurt him. She'd shut the door anyway, so he couldn't go down to her, couldn't disturb her.

She walked along the street. Waded through the snow. Looked up at the stars and the moon. If she put her mind to it enough, she could convince herself she was walking in the snow with Jason by her side, back before things went to shit with him, back before she knew what a monster he was.

Or with Dad.

Or with Max.

She imagined a combination of all of them and felt comforted for just a moment.

Imagination could be a powerful thing.

She walked until the clear sky started to shift from jet black to deep-sea blue, and she figured it was time to head back. She was freezing. Colder than she'd ever felt. Kayleigh would be worrying about her. As too would Rex.

She went to head back to them, went to walk through the front door, when she heard something up the street.

Movement.

Footsteps.

She looked around.

And for a moment, she swore she saw someone there in the street.

She blinked a few times, wondering whether it was just the product of her tired imagination.

When she looked again, he was nowhere to be seen.

She swallowed a lump in her throat and stepped back inside the house.

Looked over her shoulder once again.

She couldn't shake the feeling someone was watching.

CHAPTER FOUR

When she stepped back inside the house, Aoife knew something was wrong right away.

Something about the atmosphere of the place had changed. She couldn't put her finger on it. But something just felt missing. Something just felt... wrong.

And she had a feeling of what it was immediately. The silence. The lack of any kind of noise.

And the feeling that this house wasn't as she'd left it.

Like somebody had been here.

Like something had happened.

She felt her heart start to beat fast. Felt butterflies in her stomach and chest, fluttering quicker and quicker.

She stared into the darkness. Down the dark hallway, right over to the kitchen door. It was open. Ajar. Was it ajar when she left? She wasn't sure. She didn't think so.

But fuck, she didn't know.

She walked down the hallway. Keeping as light on her feet as she possibly could.

Because something was wrong, and she knew it.

She walked over to the lounge door. Stopped right before it.

Heart thumping faster. Sweat trickling down her burning face, even though the air was freezing.

She reached for the handle with her shaking hand, fully expecting to find someone in there.

Someone in there with Kayleigh.

With Rex.

She felt her jaw clench. Tightened her grip around that cold metal handle.

Here goes nothing...

And then she lowered it and stepped into the dark lounge.

The lounge was as she remembered it. A cracked television in the corner. Old photographs of a family lining the mantlepiece: a child in a school photo; two parents, a boy and a girl on a beach somewhere. In the corner of the room, a little fabric bag of squeaky dog toys, untouched for a long time.

The curtains were closed, so the room was dark.

But there was something glaringly clear about this room.

There was nobody in here. No intruders.

But also, no sign of Kayleigh.

Her stomach turned. She'd had a bad feeling that something might be wrong the second she'd stepped in here. She didn't know what gave her that feeling, but something was clearly off.

And now she was in here, she could see something was wrong for herself.

Kayleigh was nowhere to be seen.

Kayleigh was gone.

She thought about calling for her. There was a simple explanation to this. She was probably somewhere else in the house. Probably in the bathroom.

Or maybe she'd gone out, too. Maybe she'd noticed Aoife had gone out, and she'd tried to follow her. Or tried to simply get some space of her own. It wouldn't be the first time Kayleigh disappeared for a while, only to turn up out of nowhere.

But something felt different about this.

Something felt... off.

She stepped out of the lounge. Tried to tell herself to keep her composure. She was getting ahead of herself. She was worrying unnecessarily. Everything was going to be okay.

She walked down the hallway into the kitchen. Nobody in there. And no signs that anyone had been here, either.

The old pots beside the sink, covered in mould. The car keys sitting on the table, never to be touched again. The smell of off milk, hanging in the air.

But no sign of Kayleigh.

She stepped out of the kitchen and saw movement right at the bottom of the stairs.

She froze. Solid. Reached for her knife right away, then realised she didn't have it on her. Shit. What was she thinking? Going out without her knife? She really must not be with it tonight.

She walked back, slowly, quietly. Opened the creaky kitchen drawer, trying to keep it as silent as possible. Shuffled around for a knife while at the same time keeping her focus on that doorway, on that darkness.

She'd seen something there.

Or some*one* there.

She took a few deep breaths. Tried not to slip into anxiety. It was no good when she slipped into anxiety. She lost control of herself. Of her thoughts. Of her actions. Of everything.

She had to ride the waves. She had to feel her heartbeat and let it slow down on its own without stepping in. She had to let the fear sit there and watch it rather than get involved in it or try pushing it away.

She had to just go with it.

You've got this. You're strong. And you're quick. Anyone in here and you'll sort them in a heartbeat.

She started walking slowly. Right towards the hallway. Then

towards the foot of the stairs. And a sudden sinking feeling hit her in the stomach.

Rex.

Rex was upstairs.

He was upstairs, and whoever was in here was going up the stairs towards him.

She walked a bit quicker. Started climbing the stairs, trying to stay focused ahead, squinting into the darkness, knife in hand. She had to be careful. She knew where the creaks on these stairs were. She knew how to avoid them.

She reached the top of the stairs, the sound of her pulse racing in her ears the only thing she could hear.

She squinted around in the darkness, at the bathroom door, at the first bedroom door, and the second one…

The one where she'd slept.

And the one where Rex would be.

There was something different about this room.

There was something off about it.

The door was open.

She'd shut the door. She'd definitely shut the door. She knew she had because she always shut the door whenever she was leaving Rex, mostly so he couldn't disturb Kayleigh. She didn't distrust Kayleigh. But she knew she wasn't majorly keen on Rex. And she sometimes worried her distaste towards him might be bad news for him one of these days.

But that door. That bedroom door was open.

Something was wrong.

She thought about all the possibilities. There was no sign of Kayleigh. The door was open. And as far as she was aware, there was no sign of Rex, either.

And there was someone in this house.

There was someone here.

She climbed further up the stairs. Felt her awareness broadening. Every sound inside and outside the house grew louder. The creaking of the roof in the howling wind. The air felt cooler. Her body felt shakier. She felt exposed.

But as she stood there, shaking, she knew there was only one thing she could do. Only one place she could go.

She walked towards the bedroom door. Glanced to her left and right. She couldn't shake the feeling that someone was going to jump out from nowhere and attack her.

But there was nobody about.

The other doors were closed.

She stood in front of that ajar bedroom door. She had all sorts of visions of what she might find. All kinds of images.

Kayleigh.

Rex.

Blood...

No.

She swallowed a thick lump in her throat.

You've got this.

And then she pushed the door open further and stepped inside.

There was no sign of anybody in here.

Nobody on the bed.

Nobody around the side of the bed, by the window.

Nobody at all.

A coldness settled over Aoife. Because her fears had been confirmed.

She didn't know who, why, or where.

But then she saw the patch of blood on the bed, and her fear and her uncertainty turned to terror.

The blood on the bed.

The bloody prints out of the room, all over the carpet, towards the bedroom door.

She stared at those prints, and she heard the screaming in her mind getting louder and louder...

The power source.

The pistol.

Yuri and Kayleigh and Rex and—

No!

She closed her eyes. Held her breath. Panic completely in control now.

She was going to die.

Her heart was racing so fast she was going to die and she couldn't breathe and she wanted to puke and she couldn't move and—

Then, out of nowhere, Aoife heard something.

From the wardrobe, right behind her.

Something creaked.

Something was moving in there.

Someone was here.

CHAPTER FIVE

oife heard movement from inside the wardrobe, and she knew she wasn't alone.

She turned around. Squinted into the darkness, over to that tall white wardrobe opposite. There was someone in there. There was someone in there, and they were peeking out at her through the crack in the middle.

They were watching her.

She lifted her knife. Held it up with her shaking hand. The blood on the bed. The bloody prints leading out of the room all adding up to something awful.

Kayleigh was gone. Rex was gone.

And there were bloody prints on the bed leading out of the bedroom, and someone was here.

Here in the wardrobe.

She stared ahead. Her entire body shook. She felt so sick she could vomit. The moonlight peeked in through the window. Everything looked devoid of colour and life, black and white.

She stood there, totally frozen. She'd heard that movement, heard that creak. The unmistakable sound of someone here. Someone in the house.

And she thought of her trip up the street just before. She felt like someone was watching her. Felt like she wasn't alone.

Could've sworn she'd seen someone out there in the snow.

Kayleigh's kidnapper?

Kayleigh herself?

Or someone else?

She heard her teeth chattering and clenched her jaw to stop them. She could see her breath in front of her. But right now, she didn't feel cold. She felt warm. Suffocatingly hot.

She knew what she had to do. This was like a nightmare. One of those dreams where the painful inevitability of what was going to happen next lay right before her, taunting her.

She had to go over to that wardrobe.

She had to open those wardrobe doors.

And she had to face whoever was in there, waiting for her.

A splitting headache cracked through her skull.

A flash of memories.

Of the pistol.

Of the power source.

Of Yuri and Kayleigh.

Of pulling the trigger and...

That noise.

That noise burning through her skull.

The splitting pain of white noise so loud it made her ears ache.

Don't think about that. Don't remember that.

Resist it. Push it away.

You won't resist it forever, Aoife.

"No," she gasped.

She opened her eyes.

Clutched the knife tight.

There was only one thing she could do here, and she had to do it now.

She took a deep breath.

Tried to steady her racing heart.

Tried to ignore the sirens circling her mind.

You've got this.

Everything's going to be okay.

Everything's...

She opened the wardrobe doors and lifted her knife.

Darkness stared back at her.

Nothing but darkness. Old boots. Suits and jumpers that looked like they'd been attacked by moths.

But there was no one in the wardrobe.

She took another deep breath. Felt herself growing calmer and calmer by the second. Stupid bitch. She was imagining things. It was all in her head. She was getting spooked 'cause of Kayleigh and Rex going missing, and she was imagining things.

She needed to get a grip. She couldn't go losing her shit. Not now.

She needed to focus on what really mattered here. On what was most important.

Finding Kayleigh. Finding Rex.

She walked away from the wardrobe, looking into the darkness one last time, when she heard footsteps running across the hall outside.

She froze. Completely still. Heart started picking up again. Hands started shaking again.

Someone was out there.

She stood there, not moving a muscle. *You're wrong. You thought someone was in the wardrobe, and they weren't. You're hearing things. That's all this is.*

But she heard that movement. Creeping across the hall outside. The floorboards creaking.

And there was no denying it.

There was someone out there.

She walked to the bedroom door. Keeping as light on her feet as she could.

She got to it. Lowered the handle. Eased it open.

This is a bad dream. This has to be a bad dream.

She opened the door and looked out onto the hallway.

There was nobody there.

Nothing but darkness.

She stood there for a few seconds. The doors were all closed. There was no sign of anybody. She was losing her shit. She was actually going crazy.

She shook her head. She'd gone this route before. Didn't want to go this route again. The sinking feeling in the pit of her stomach that she might actually be imagining all this. That it might be in her head.

She took a few deep breaths. Tried to focus on what she knew was real, and what she knew was right here in front of her.

Her breathing.

One thing she could be sure of.

And when she stepped out of the bedroom, she suddenly heard something behind her.

More movement.

She stopped.

Because suddenly, it dawned on her.

The movement.

It wasn't in the bedroom.

It wasn't in the wardrobe.

And it wasn't in the hall.

She looked up at the ceiling.

Looked at the hatch leading towards the attic.

Every muscle in her body went weak.

Somebody was up there.

Somebody was in the attic.

She wasn't alone in this house.

CHAPTER SIX

oife stared up at the entrance to the attic and listened to the movement above.

There was somebody up there. She was absolutely certain of it. She could hear creaking footsteps every now and then. And it all made sense. The sound she thought she'd heard in the wardrobe. Then in the hall here.

It came from above.

There was someone up there.

She stared up at that attic entrance. The white painted hatch leading up towards the darkness above. She knew it was risky just opening that attic door. She knew she needed to be careful. Very careful. The second she opened that attic door, someone could be waiting up there. Waiting to jump down and attack her.

They could have a gun. They could have *anything*.

She needed to be very, very careful.

She thought about just leaving. Walking away. She didn't need to know who was up there or what they were doing. And if it wasn't for Kayleigh and Rex's disappearance, maybe she could have just walked away without her curiosity getting the better of her.

But she couldn't walk away now. Not if whoever was up there in the attic had something to do with Kayleigh and Rex going missing in any way.

What if they haven't gone missing? What if they've just gone for a walk? What if they've just gone to get some air, just like you did?

No. Aoife knew deep down that wasn't true. It couldn't be.

There was something else going on here that she just couldn't quite put her finger on.

She reached up with her shaking hand. Held the button that would release the attic door and send the hatch swinging down towards her.

She needed to be calm.

Focused.

Ready.

She took a deep breath and closed her eyes.

Keep your shit together.

And then she pushed that button.

The hatch swung open.

Dust filled her eyes, made her sneeze.

She covered her face and raised her knife, waiting for whatever assailant was up there to jump down and ambush her.

Waiting.

Waiting.

Waiting.

But nobody jumped down.

Nobody ambushed her.

She rubbed her eyes, squinted above in that darkness.

Still nobody.

Not even a sound anymore.

She felt her throat tightening. Fuck. Part of her wanted someone to jump out at her. Because if they didn't, it meant she was more likely to have to go up there. Search up there for herself.

She looked around at the staircase.

You can walk away.

You can walk away from this place, and you can leave.

But no. She couldn't. Because Kayleigh and Rex...

You know deep down you can walk away.

You know you can walk away because—

She reached for the ladders. Dragged them down.

Constantly on edge. Constantly aware of any noise that might come from above. Of anyone that may come leaping down towards her.

Heart racing.

Head spinning.

It didn't matter what she told herself. It didn't matter how much she tried to convince herself.

She was going up that ladder and into the attic.

She climbed the creaky steps. The air seemed to turn even colder as she got closer and closer towards that dark opening. She couldn't hear anything up there anymore. Any movement, or anything like that.

And that scared her even more. Because it meant she didn't know where whoever was up there was.

She climbed so close to the void, to the brink of total darkness. Fully expecting someone to jump out and stab her in the neck before she had a chance to enter.

She had to do this quickly.

She waited just a few seconds.

And then she hurried up the last few steps and into the attic.

It was pitch black. So dusty. Cold and damp.

But she was in here.

She was in here, and she was alive.

She was in here, and nobody had ambushed her.

She stayed still. Very still. Squinted around in the darkness. Looked for movement. Looked for a sign of life.

But she couldn't see a thing.

The outlines of old boxes, one for a television, another for a

Playstation. A Christmas tree and its accompanying decorations lost to the darkness. Tons of clothing, all coated in a thick layer of dust and grime.

No movement at all. No sounds at all.

And then, in the corner of her eye, she saw something shift.

She turned. Raised her knife.

She wanted to call out. Shout out.

But at the same time... she wanted to keep as low a profile as possible.

She crept over towards the source of that movement, slowly. Again, she couldn't see them moving anymore. Couldn't hear anything either.

She just got closer and closer to its source, and she stopped.

There was a pile of boxes right in front of her.

Whoever was in this attic was right behind those boxes.

She put her weight against it, just gently. They weren't heavy boxes. But she'd be able to push them over and stun whoever was at the side, at least momentarily.

She gulped. Leaned against them gently.

She had to be ready.

She had to time this right.

She gritted her teeth as she stood there in the darkness and waited for the perfect moment.

No time like the fucking present, Aoife. Now or never...

And then she leaned against the boxes.

Pushed them over. Right onto whoever was behind them.

And then she launched herself around the side of the boxes, knife raised.

First, she heard a whimper.

A cry.

A childlike scream.

She stopped. Held back.

Squinted into the darkness at the spot just behind the boxes.

She still couldn't make out shapes properly in the darkness.

But she could see something very clearly.

Someone was lying right in front of her in this attic.

And it wasn't what she expected.

A little boy.

Lying under the boxes.

Sniffing. Crying.

Hand raised.

"Please don't hurt me," he said. "Please."

CHAPTER SEVEN

"Please don't hurt me. Please don't hurt me. Please."

Aoife stood in the attic and stared down into the darkness at the boy before her. She couldn't see his face. She could barely make out the colour of his hair. She could just see the outline of his body in the darkness. Small. Looked smaller than a teenager, even. Sounded young, too.

"Don't hurt me. Don't—don't hurt me. Please."

She swallowed a lump in her throat. She didn't know what to say. Finding a kid up here wasn't exactly what she expected. Not something you came across in your bloody attic every day, right?

And besides. Finding *anyone* in these circumstances was always going to be a difficult one. Because Aoife was confused. She didn't understand.

And she was afraid.

"What... How..." She tried speaking. Tried saying something. But she couldn't find the words. What did anyone say in a situation like this?

But the kid just didn't stop begging. "Don't hurt me. I don't... I don't want to be hurt. Not again. Not again."

She heard him crying. Sobbing away on this attic floor. And

even though she'd gone out of her way to avoid people this past eighteen months, she knew it was a bit of a faux pas leaving a kid sobbing on the floor like this.

But at the same time, she had to be careful. Because this was no ordinary situation.

"Are you alone?" Aoife asked.

The kid kept on crying.

"Hey," Aoife said. "I asked you a question. Are you alone?"

"Yes," the boy said. Sniffing.

It felt weird interacting with someone who wasn't Kayleigh. Even hearing her own voice speaking to someone else sounded unusual. Unnatural.

"What's your name?"

The boy cried. Like he kept on forgetting she was even there.

Aoife knew she would have to take on a softer tone if she wanted to win this boy's trust. She'd been isolated from the outside world so much that she'd forgotten all rules when it came to interacting with other people.

She crouched down. As much as it felt dangerous. As much as it made her feel uncomfortable.

"I'm... I'm Aoife," she said. "What's your name?"

The boy sniffed a few times again. Cleared his throat. "Billy."

"Billy," Aoife said. "It's... it's nice to meet you, Billy. Wish it could've been in better circumstances. But..."

She stopped. Who the hell was she speaking to right now? A kid or a client? She was really fucking rusty on a socialising front, that was for sure.

"How long have you been up here, Billy?"

"I don't know," Billy said.

She realised she'd asked a stupid question. How was the kid supposed to know how long he'd been up here? What did that question even mean anymore, anyway? Without a way of comprehensively measuring time, what use was a question like that anymore?

"I've seen... I've seen light outside twice. I think. So maybe... maybe this is the third night."

Wow. Three nights he'd been up here. Come to think of it, that explained the sounds she thought she'd heard. Thought it was just Kayleigh or Rex. Or something in her mind.

But now this kid, Billy. Right here in the attic.

Explained a lot.

"I just... I just don't want to hurt no more," Billy said. "I'll be no trouble. I just... I just need to hide out here a bit longer. I won't get in your way. Please."

Hearing him say these things, Aoife felt sorry for the lad. He sounded so grown up for a kid of his age. Couldn't be much older than ten, surely?

But the way he spoke, the things he said... you'd expect a kid in need to be begging for help.

Instead, he was just begging Aoife to let him stay up here.

She heard what he was saying about being hurt, too. And what that implied. Someone was hurting him. Someone was doing nasty things to him. And she felt bitter about that, even though she didn't know the lad. No kid deserved to go through hell.

"Who's hurting you?" Aoife asked.

Billy cried some more. "Please. Just let me stay here."

"If you're gonna stay here, I need to know who's been hurting you. And where you've come from."

She saw Billy look at her. Even though it was dark, she could tell her was staring at her, scanning her, trying to figure out whether he could trust her.

"It's not a trick question," Aoife said. "I just want to know what's led you to this attic. Staying up here. It's freezing up here. Wherever you came from... it can't have been nice for you to want to get away so bad."

"It was horrible," Billy said.

Aoife swallowed a lump in her throat. "Where?"

"I don't know where," Billy said. "Just that they didn't treat me nice. Or the other kids nice. The men there, they... they did things to us. Bad things. Please. Don't let them get me again. Don't make me go back there."

Aoife felt sick. Rage built up inside. Poor kid. She knew there were some nasty fuckers about. She wasn't naive. But it sounded like this kid had been the victim of some nasty shit.

He'd got away. Escaped. And good on him.

She just wished there was more she could do for him.

She just wished she wasn't so afraid.

And then she remembered Kayleigh and Rex, and she knew she needed to find them. Urgently.

"While you were up here," Aoife said. "I left the house a bit ago for a walk. Did you hear anything happen? Anyone come in here looking for you? Or did you hear anyone leave? My friend? A dog?"

The dark silhouette stared up at her.

White noise stung her ears, getting louder and louder, like static.

Don't say it don't say it don't—

"No," Billy said. "I didn't hear anything."

Aoife nodded, somewhat relieved. She thought about the bloody footprints and the blood on the bed. Kayleigh and Rex, nowhere to be seen.

But at least the kid hadn't heard any signs of struggle.

And at least he hadn't heard...

She told herself to be calm. Because they'd be okay. Wherever Kayleigh and Rex were, she'd find them, and they'd be okay.

She walked over to the hatch. Then looked back at Billy. She felt sorry for him. Didn't want to leave him up here on his own.

But at the same time...

"If you need anything," Aoife said. "A blanket, or food, or whatever. Just give me a knock. Okay?"

She saw Billy's shadowy head nod.

Smiled at him. Feeling guilty for being so cold. So distant.

"And if I'm out, just help yourself. There's somewhere I need to be. So just help yourself and keep a low profile. I'm sure you'll be okay here. Right?"

"Thank you," Billy said.

A knot in Aoife's stomach. Twisting insides.

Eyes welling up.

"It's okay," she said.

She wanted to tell him to come down the ladder with her.

She wanted so much to open up and let him in.

But then she turned around.

Climbed down the ladder.

She reached the hall floor and stood there and couldn't quite believe the exchange she'd just had was real. It couldn't be real.

Could it?

She was about to push the ladders back up when she heard something outside.

Voices in the street.

She walked into the front bedroom. Over to the window.

Outside, she saw people in the street.

Men.

Men holding knives, baseball bats, and all types of weapons.

"Wherever the little shit went, he can't have gone fucking far," one of them said.

She looked down at these men, illuminated in the moonlight, and she realised who they were.

The men who Billy had escaped.

They'd actually come after him.

Her heart started racing. Her body tensed up. She hadn't signed up for this crap. She just wanted to live an easy life. A life on her own. A life...

That's when one of the men looked right up through the window.

Looked right into her eyes.

Time stood still.

He hadn't seen her. He couldn't have seen her. She was imagining things. He'd keep on looking around, and they'd walk on, and this wouldn't be a problem.

But then she saw him lift a hand.

Point right at the window and right at her.

And then he and his people started running towards the house.

CHAPTER EIGHT

Aoife saw the men on the street running towards the house she was inside, and she knew right away she had to hide.

She turned around and looked at the bedroom, taking in her surroundings in one. The wardrobe? Under the bed? No. No, she had to go somewhere quieter. She had to go somewhere they wouldn't find her—and somewhere she'd still have the upper ground if they did.

She knew a place matching that description perfectly.

The attic.

The attic, where Billy was hiding.

She knew there was no time to waste. She had to get the fuck out of this bedroom and get the fuck up that ladder right this second.

She ran across the bedroom floor towards that ladder leading up to the attic, and she heard the front door creak open.

She froze on the spot. Stared up at that ladder and up into the darkness above. She hadn't had a chance to push the ladder up or close the attic door. Billy was up there—and the ladder being down and the door being open drew attention to the attic.

But those footsteps creaking up the stairs.

Those voices.

"Don't let her fucking leave. She must've seen something."

She stood at the door, and she knew she had literally seconds to act.

Seconds to decide what to do.

She wanted to protect Billy.

She didn't want the ladder to the attic to be open like that, drawing attention to him.

But she knew she didn't have time to do anything about it.

So she ran out of the bedroom and into the spare room at the front of the house.

She threw herself into the wardrobe. Pulled the door shut behind her. Heard those footsteps running up the stairs. Two of them, at least.

All of them rushing for the front bedroom. The one she'd just run out of.

She waited. Held her breath. Couldn't fucking breathe if she wanted to. She had to wait until they were in that bedroom.

And then she had to run up into the attic.

She had to run up there and get to Billy, and she had to get out of here.

She heard the footsteps creaking around the bedroom. Heard the men slamming wardrobe doors open. Heard them banging about, searching the place.

"She's not fucking here."

"She's got to be here somewhere."

"Are you sure you even saw anyone?"

"I know what the fuck I saw, okay?"

"Check the attic. She mighta run up there. Ladder being down and all that."

Aoife's stomach sank.

They were going to go up there.

They were going to go up there, and they were going to find Billy.

She heard one of the men walking out the bedroom into the hall.

Then she heard his feet climbing the ladder.

She listened, and she kept still, so still.

Think, Aoife. Think.

She waited until he was at the top of the ladder. Half-expected a scream, right away, from Billy. A cry from the boy. And the thought of it filled her with horror. The poor kid had been through enough. He didn't deserve any of it. And he definitely didn't deserve to be taken back to the hell he'd escaped.

The man's footsteps stopped.

She heard his weight shift to the attic above.

Heard him creaking around up there.

And she knew it was her time to do something.

She stepped out of the wardrobe. Clutched her knife in hand. Stopped right away.

A man with long, dark hair, sighing, descending the stairs. He must be the other guy. The one from the bedroom.

She glanced to her right. Looked into the bedroom the two men had gone. Didn't see anybody in there.

Which meant she was clear.

She had a chance.

A chance to climb that ladder.

A chance to get up to the attic.

A chance to help Billy.

She waited for the man to reach the bottom of the stairs, waited until she heard him talking to other people outside, and she rushed across the hall towards the ladders.

She grabbed the ladder, started to climb. She could hear shuffling up there.

Hold on, Billy. You'll be okay.

She climbed another step when she suddenly flew forward.

Her forehead cracked against the metal step.

And then a hand grabbed her neck and dragged her back down onto the floor.

She lay on her back and looked up.

A man. Not the long-haired one who she'd seen leave the place. Another one. Ginger. Spotty face. Yellow teeth.

Holding her by the throat.

"Hello, miss," he said. "Where d'you think you're goin'?"

She swung her knife towards him.

He punched it away. Pinned her wrist down. Held it tight. Smiled.

"I don't think so," he said.

It was right then that she heard something from above.

Billy's scream.

CHAPTER NINE

Aoife heard Billy's scream from above and knew he'd been found.

The man above her pinned her down by the throat. Squeezed so tightly around her neck that the blood pumping through it felt like it was going to burst out. Bright colours filled her eyes. She couldn't breathe. She could hear shuffling and strug gling above, and she knew Billy had no chance. He was small, and he was weak, and they'd found him. The very people he'd fled— presumably—had found him.

And there was nothing she could do to help him.

She tried to take a swing at the man, but his right hand was around her wrist. So tight it felt it might break. The full weight of his body pressed down on her belly. Anxiety hit. The sudden realisation that she was going to suffocate here. She was going to suffocate, and she was going to die on the floor here in this house.

She wished Kayleigh was here. She wished Rex was here.

She wished someone was here to help her.

Sounds grew muffled as she tried to shake herself free of this man's grip. Her arms and legs started tingling, a lightness taking over. She realised with another burst of crippling fear that she was going to fall unconscious. She was going to pass out. And God knows where she'd wake up.

God knows whether she'd ever wake up again.

She tried with what little strength she had left to break free of his grip. Kicked out. Tried to punch him with her free hand. But it was just no good.

He leaned right into her. Whispered in her ear with his hot, rancid breath. "We're gonna have a lotta fun with you, missy. A lotta fun indeed…"

She felt him turn her head around onto its side. Push it into the floor, right against the rough carpet.

And then she saw it.

The cabinet.

The cabinet up against the wall.

The heavy-looking statue of someone historically famous Aoife should probably be aware of sitting on top of it.

She stretched out as far as she could. As far as her aching body would allow. Tried to get to it before the colours filled her eyes completely. Before the tingling engulfed her.

She felt the bottom of the cabinet touch the tips of her fingers, and for a moment, just a moment, she felt hope.

And then she felt his grip around her throat loosen.

She grabbed her other arm.

"I don't think so," he said.

He pinned down both arms, now. So her throat was free. She could breathe, at least. That gave her a little more time awake. Conscious. Even though her neck hurt like hell.

She felt his hands tighten around her wrists. She knew she was screwed now. She tried to lean up, to headbutt him, to wrap her teeth around his throat and tear it the hell off—whatever it took to break free of him.

But there was nothing.

There was no way out.

She lay there, and she found herself praying for an intervention. Because she was all out of options.

And it was right then that she heard it.

A thump.

A heavy thump from somewhere above.

The man's head suddenly jolting forward, slamming against her chest.

Something warm spilling over her.

Something she soon realised was blood.

She lay there. The man's weight still pressing down on her. She didn't know what'd happened.

She blinked a few times. Tried to make sense of the scene in front of her.

The man pinning her down lay there twitching. Blood pooled out of a huge crack wound on his head, dark blood all clotting in his ginger hair.

There was something right beside him, on the floor.

Another of those heavy ornate statues. A black metal one.

Blood on its side.

She looked at it and didn't understand. Had it fallen from above? Had it...

And then she looked up at the attic entrance and saw him.

Billy.

She'd not seen his face outside the pitch black of the attic yet. But she could just about make it out now, in this softer darkness. Deathly pale. Thin. Little sores and bruises all over it.

She looked up at him, alone up there, and realised it was silent above. He must've done something to the bloke who'd gone up for him, somehow. And then he must've pushed that statue out of the attic and right onto his head.

Aoife's first thought was that she was fucking lucky it hadn't hit *her* head. But then she figured the kid had saved her life, so she couldn't chastise him for being too reckless right now.

She pushed the man's heavy body off her. Gasped for breath as his weight shifted. Coughed a few times, then lay there on the floor for a few seconds, catching her breath, gaining some composure.

And then the urgency of the situation caught up with her again.

There was a dead man in this hall.

Billy was in the attic, and presumably, there was another guy up there in not great condition.

And outside, there were more of these people.

She stood up. Reached for Billy.

"We need to get out of here," she said.

Billy's eyes widened. He shook his head. "But—but if they catch me—"

"There's more chance of them catching you if you stay up there. Trust me, kid. We need to get out of here, right now."

He looked at her. Stared at her. Like he was trying to weigh up whether he could trust her.

And then he nodded.

He climbed down the ladders slowly. She could see blood on his hands, and she knew something had happened up there. She didn't want to ask him what. But whatever he'd done, he'd saved himself, and he'd saved her too.

She could see his slim frame even better now. Like someone from one of those old Children in Need ads back in the day. So fragile. So frail. Maybe not as young as she'd first thought, but looking younger for the state he was in.

He reached the floor, looked at the twitching body of the man lying there, a desensitised glaze to his eyes.

And then he walked over to Aoife's side. Got close to her.

She looked at him for a second. Right into his innocent little eyes.

"Come on," she said. "We've got to figure out a way out of here. Before they..."

"What's takin' you guys so long?"

A voice downstairs. A shout.

The front door creaking open.

Footsteps.

"Michael," the man shouted. "What the hell's goin' on up there?"

She stared at Billy. He stared back at her. Both of them frozen. Silent.

Don't come in. Please don't come in.

And then she heard someone entering the house.

"Michael! What the hell you doing?"

Another pause.

Aoife holding her breath.

Please turn back. Please...

Then, footsteps creaking up the stairs.

CHAPTER TEN

A oife heard the footsteps creaking up the stairs and knew her and Billy had to get the fuck out of here.

Fast.

Those footsteps got closer and closer. They weren't slowing down. Soon, whoever it was would be in this hall, and they were going to find the body, and then they were going to go up into the attic and presumably find *another* body...

Aoife knew she had to act fast.

She grabbed Billy's hand and ran into the bathroom, right at the back of the house.

She rushed over to the window. Past the bath, which was filled with mould and grime. Over to the frosted window, which she prayed to God was unlocked...

Her prayers weren't answered.

It was locked.

"Damn it," Aoife said.

She heard something, then. The man's voice. "Shit!"

And she knew he'd found the body.

She knew he'd found the body, and she knew they were going to find her and Billy.

She ran over to the bathroom door. Slammed it shut. Locked it.

"Billy, we're going to need to break this window and jump out the back."

Billy's eyes widened. He looked scared. But he just nodded. Like he knew it was the only thing they could do.

It made her feel sad, seeing how compliant he was. She had no idea what kind of suffering he'd been put through to push him to that point. She didn't want to think about it.

She looked around the bathroom for something heavy she could use. Something she could throw at the window to smash it. She couldn't see anything. Nothing by the sink. Nothing by the old bath. Nothing at all.

Think, Aoife. Think.

She looked over at the toilet, and suddenly it clicked.

The toilet tank cover.

She could use that.

She went to grab it when she heard a bang on the door.

And then another.

And another.

The door rattling against the lock.

The lock looked tough, but it wasn't going to hold. Not for long.

"Open the fuck up!"

Aoife ignored it as best she could. She had to focus now. Total focus on getting the fuck out of this bathroom and getting Billy out of this bathroom.

She ran over to the toilet tank cover, grabbed it, and then she took a swing at the window with it.

A crack.

A crack, right in the middle of it.

But still not enough to break it fully.

"Aoife!"

She looked around. Saw Billy staring back at the bathroom

door.

There was a hole in it.

A hole where someone was whacking against it with a hammer.

"They're going to get in," Billy said. "They're going to get in and take me back."

Shit. They were close. So fucking close.

She turned back around and pulled back the toilet lid cover. One more hit. That had to do it.

And then they could focus on jumping the hell out of this window.

She swung at the glass.

It smashed before her. Exploded into little shards, raining over everywhere.

That was something, at least.

She dropped the toilet tank cover and brushed aside some of the loose glass. The drop wasn't too bad. They could drop onto the extension at the back of the house, then onto the garden, and then they could jump the fences and be out of here.

But they had to be quick about it.

Another crack at the bathroom door.

"Don't even think about running, Billy. You know how much trouble you'll be in if you run!"

Aoife looked around. The door was mostly torn away now. It'd be breached in no time.

Hearing the anger in that man's voice. Seeing it in his blood-shot eyes.

"Don't you dare run, Billy. You know what happens to runners. Don't make this any worse for yourself."

Aoife felt white-hot anger towards this man.

She wanted to walk over to him and stab him in the fucking throat for even implying what he was implying. But she'd left her knife in the hall outside, and she didn't have anything to defend herself with right now.

And besides. Time was running out.

"Out the window, Billy," Aoife said. "Come on."

She looked around. Stood beside him as he climbed out, trying to avoid the sharp shards of glass from cutting him. And then, when he was on the edge of the window ledge, dangling down, he looked up at her with pitiful but trusting eyes.

"Will I be okay?"

She smiled at him. "You'll be okay. I promise you'll be okay."

He nodded.

"Go on. You've got this. Trust me."

He nodded again.

Took a deep breath.

Then he dropped onto the roof of the extension below.

He landed with a thud, and tumbled forward. Got back to his feet and looked up at her as he stood there. Smile on his face. Like he was proud. And she was proud of him too.

I'm coming. We're getting out of this.

She went to climb out of the window and jump down after him when suddenly, she heard an awful creaking noise, right below.

The extension roof.

Something was wrong.

Billy looked down at the roof.

"Billy!" she shouted. "Get off there! Now!"

But it was already too late.

The extension roof collapsed.

And Billy fell into the abyss below.

CHAPTER ELEVEN

Aoife watched as Billy fell through the extension roof, and her entire world stood still.

He'd jumped down there, and he'd disappeared. The roof had just caved in beneath him.

And now he was in there. Trapped in there. Probably hurt. Possibly not even alive anymore...

No. She couldn't think like that.

She had to get down there, and she had to get to him, and she had to get him the hell out of this place.

Especially before these people chasing him got to him.

She went to climb out the window when suddenly, she heard an enormous crack behind her.

She looked back.

The man bashing at the door with his hammer was breaking into the bathroom.

Halfway through the door, which he'd made good work of.

"Don't you move a muscle," he said. "Don't you fucking dare."

She knew she could have made a run for it. She knew she could have jumped down below to get to Billy. Because she couldn't fuck about anymore. Time was of the essence.

But this guy, what he'd said about Billy, what he'd implied...

She wasn't letting this fucker get away.

So before he could get himself fully through the door, she grabbed the toilet tank cover.

Pulled it back.

"You're not going anywhere," she said.

And then she swung it at his chin.

Hard.

His chin cracked. His head flipped back, and he fell back, twitching and spluttering.

She dropped the blood-soaked toilet tank cover.

Turned to the window.

She'd dealt with that fucker.

Now, she just had to get to Billy.

She dropped out of the window, into the cold, onto a section of the extension roof that seemed more stable. Crept over to the opening where Billy had fallen. She could hear voices at the front of the house. Commotion kicking up. She had to get to Billy quickly, or they'd be onto him.

She shuffled around to the edge of the opening below. Squinted down, tried to see Billy amidst the dusty darkness.

"Fuck it. No choice."

She held her breath then dropped down into the darkness below.

She looked around the extension. Little table in the middle, which was surrounded by debris. Old board games stacked in the corner of the room. A television on the wall.

But no sign of Billy.

Footsteps behind. Shouting.

They were in the house.

More of them were in the house, and they were coming.

"Billy?" she called. Part of her hoped he'd made a dash for it already. At least that way, he might be okay.

She looked around the darkness of the conservatory and suddenly saw him right there.

A doorway.

A doorway leading to the garage.

Standing there. Cut. Bruised. Bleeding from his head.

But he was okay.

"Thank God," she said. "I'm sorry. I had no idea. I thought the roof would hold. I had no idea."

He nodded. So compliant. So forgiving.

And yet, a little less trusting.

She ran over to him. Closed the door gently. And then she ran into the garage. Past the table tennis table right in the middle, the snooker table, and right over to the garage door.

"Almost there," she said, opening it up. "Almost…"

As she lifted the door, she heard voices outside. Footsteps. Movement. They weren't all in the house. Not yet.

"Wait," she said. "Just a little longer."

She lowered her head. Peeked out of that crack beneath the garage. Heard the voices in the house. And heard more of them outside, too.

She looked out at the front garden.

At the pair of feet heading towards the house.

Waited for them to disappear from view.

Heard the door to the garage open, right on cue.

"Now," Aoife said.

She lifted the garage door. Pushed Billy outside. And then climbed under the gap herself.

As she turned around, she saw three men flooding into that garage.

"Stop! At the front! Stop them!"

She slammed the garage door shut.

And then she grabbed Billy's hand.

She didn't look at the front door.

She didn't look to see if there were any more of them around.

She just gripped his hand as tight as she could, and she ran off down the road, through the snow, away from the shouting voices, and into the darkness.

CHAPTER TWELVE

Aoife didn't stop running until she was absolutely sure nobody was following her.

Her and Billy were alongside a canal. The water was frozen over completely. Could probably walk on it, but after Billy went tumbling through a frigging roof earlier, she didn't want to take any chances on that front. They'd rode their luck more than enough today.

She walked down this canal path, constantly aware of her surroundings. Every noise, every bit of movement, she was so conscious of. Those people chasing her and Billy. They didn't seem the type to give up. Especially not after what they'd done to their people.

"Don't you dare run, Billy. You know what happens to runners. Don't make this any worse for yourself."

She thought of those words, and she felt herself shudder. God knows what they'd put this poor kid through if they got him back. It didn't bear thinking about.

She looked at him, fully visible in the moonlight now. The sky was getting a bit lighter, too, as morning approached. He was a pitiful little thing. Wearing torn, grey pyjamas, which dangled off his bony frame. Blue lips and fingertips. Little bruises across his face. He was shivering. Really bad.

"I'd offer you a coat," Aoife said, realising how cold he was—and how damned cold *she* was, for that matter. "But I didn't really have the chance to grab one on our way out."

He glanced up at her, then looked away. Kid clearly had trust issues. Couldn't blame him.

"You'll be okay now. They won't find you here. You'll be safe from them. We both will."

Billy nodded again, but Aoife got the sense he wasn't convinced. Which she could understand. When you'd been through hell, it felt like it'd follow you everywhere. Like there was no hiding from it.

She still wasn't sure she'd outrun the demons of her past herself.

"I know you're tired," Aoife said. "But we need to keep moving. To keep warm. And then find someplace to lay low for a while. To grab some rest. We'll freeze to death out here. Need to get in front of a fire somewhere. How's that sound?"

He glanced up at her again, then looked away. Nodded. Wasn't a boy of many words. Again, she got it. He'd probably been through so much hell at the hands of adults that he didn't trust anyone at this point.

She walked along this canal path with him, keeping her focus on her surroundings at all times. "Where'd... where'd you come from originally?"

"Nottingham," Billy said.

"Nice. I used to know a Forest fan."

He looked up at her like he didn't understand what she was talking about.

"Football," she said. "You not a fan?"

Billy shook his head. "My dad used to want me to be. I tried. But I just found it... I dunno. Boring, I guess."

Aoife smiled. "Me too. Spent a lot of years pretending I was interested in football for the sake of other people. Usually men. Quite freeing to end up in a world where it's totally and completely irrelevant now."

Billy smiled. Stared up at her, still uncertain. What the hell was she rambling on about? The kid could clearly tell she was out of social practice.

"How old are you?" Aoife asked.

"Fourteen."

"Fourteen? Wow." He looked a lot younger. Probably how thin he was. "You've done well. Surviving this long. And now you've got your whole life ahead of you. Any jobs you're interested in doing? I believe Sainsbury's are taking on new recruits."

It was meant to be a joke, but again it fell flat. Note to self: nihilistic, sarcastic jokes about the future of mankind being completely and utterly fucked were off the table with emotionally traumatised kids.

"How'd you end up... you know. With those men."

Billy kept his focus on the path. "I... I was at my grandma's when the lights went out. I got scared. Never liked the dark. Not then, anyway. I went into her room and she... she was gone."

"That's rough," Aoife said. "I'm sorry."

"I tried to find Mum and Dad, but I never did. I needed medicine. Injections. The insulin."

"You're diabetic?"

Billy shrugged. "I thought I needed it. But then... I've not had it for a long time. And I'm okay. So, I don't know."

Weird. If someone needed insulin, she was pretty sure they needed insulin for life. Which made her wonder about Billy. She didn't know why, but maybe his family hadn't been completely straight with him about what medicine he was taking or what he needed to take. Who knows?

There were some mysteries in life that would never be fully understood.

"So how'd you make it this far?" Aoife said. "Before you came across that bunch of nonces?"

"'Nonces'?"

"It's just... Don't worry. Just a word I use for people like your captors."

Billy nodded. Looked at Aoife like he found her a little strange. "I was with some nice people. They helped me. But then bad people came. We had to run away. Found another nice place, but then the same happened again. And then Ramiro's gang caught us, and since then, I've... Well, I don't know. There's been different people. Different groups. But I... I..."

"It's okay," Aoife. "You don't have to talk about it."

"What about you?" he asked. Quickly, like he was desperately trying to divert attention from himself.

"Me?"

"Where are you from? What... what's happened with you?"

Aoife thought of all of it. Max. The conflict with Grace. She thought of finding Kayleigh, and of Sanctuary, and then of Yuri, and how everything fell apart.

And then she thought of...

No.

She didn't have to think of that.

"I thought I'd found everything I needed," Aoife said. "Turns out... turns out I was wrong. But I'm still here. Right?"

"And your friends," Billy said.

"What?"

"You said your friend was with you. And your dog."

Aoife's stomach turned. Her mouth went dry. Kayleigh and Rex. Fuck. How had she let them slip from her mind? All this focus on getting away, all this focus on Billy, and she'd let her attention drift from them.

"Yeah," Aoife said. "Although sometimes I'm not entirely sure how much of a friend she is anymore."

"What do you mean by that?"

Aoife saw it all again.

The power source.

The pistol in her hand.

Yuri's gun to Kayleigh's head.

The sound of static in her skull.

"Nothing," Aoife said. "Come on. Less talking, more walking. We need to find someplace to shelter and get warm. And we need to rest."

"And then what?" Billy asked.

It was a question Aoife hadn't thought about. Hadn't even considered. But Billy was right. Then what?

Because she couldn't leave Billy on his own. He wouldn't survive out here. Not without her help.

She didn't want to befriend anyone. Didn't want the risk of losing anyone on her conscience, not again.

But she hadn't really been given much choice.

"We'll figure that out as we go," she said. "Now come on. Let's find somewhere to rest."

Billy looked up at her. And for a moment, as the moon beamed across his face, she swore she saw him smiling at her.

The pair of them walked off, further down the canal path, towards the suburbs ahead.

And as much as Aoife hated to admit it, she could feel herself bonding with this poor kid.

And she knew just how dangerous that was.

CHAPTER THIRTEEN

Ramiro saw Michael's body lying there in the middle of the landing, dark blood oozing out of his cracked skull, and he felt anger surge through his body.

Michael was in a bad way. A really fucking bad way. The baddest way of all. Dead as a fucking doorpost, if that's how the saying goes. Who cared if it wasn't how the saying went? Nobody around to play grammar nazi anymore.

There was a heavy-looking statue right beside him, blood and bits of skull and brain clinging to it. Whoever had hit him had hit him really fucking hard.

He looked down at that dent in his skull. At his brain inside. At how his eyes stared blankly, widely, into nothingness. Michael was always a good bloke. Loyal. A bit too inquisitive for his own good sometimes, something that had got the better of him in the end. But Ramiro had always been able to trust him. Always been able to rely on him. A good man, gone.

And then lying there in front of him, the other side of this ladder leading to the attic, Jimmy.

Jimmy was in an even worse state. His jaw looked like it'd been snapped clean off, dangling onto his face by a thread off flesh.

And the worst thing about poor Jimmy?

He was still alive.

He lay there. Twitching. Choking on blood. Trying to move. Trying to writhe around. Trying to stand up, even though the poor fucker was clearly paralysed. Couldn't lift himself.

Sounded like he just wanted to say something, too. Just wanted to speak.

Poor bastard.

Ramiro didn't like Jimmy as much. He was a bit of a loser and a bit of a creep. But again, he was loyal, and loyalty was the most valuable trait a person could have these days.

He looked down at poor Jimmy, lying there in the darkness, and he shook his head. "Really got yourself in a right ol' mess this time, eh Jim?"

Jimmy clutched at the air. Tried to move. Tried to speak.

Staring up at him with that half a face, like something from The Walking Dead.

"Ramiro," a voice said.

He looked up. Saw Kurt staring down at him from the attic, wide-eyed. Not a good look.

"What's up?"

Kurt turned to dodge Ramiro's gaze. "It's him."

"*He* has a name."

"It's—it's Barney."

The purple fucking dinosaur himself. One of his best friends. He wasn't actually called Barney, but he sometimes dressed up as that dinosaur to put on a show for the kids. A creep. Completely twisted.

But a good laugh. Again, loyal. Trustworthy.

And from the look on Kurt's face, dead, too.

"How'd it happen?" Ramiro asked.

"Looks like a knife wound to the throat."

Ramiro nodded. "Poor bastards."

"There's something else here, too."

He held out his hand. Dropped something down to Ramiro.

Ramiro caught it. And right away, he recognised it.

The silver pendant. The one Billy always carried. They let him hold onto it 'cause hell, it wasn't doing them any harm. And at the end of the day, they wanted the kids to feel comfortable. Their comfort meant they were more valuable, after all. It mattered that they were looked after.

He curled his fingers around the pendant. Suddenly, a clear image of what'd happened here started to play out in Ramiro's mind. Billy had hidden in the attic. He'd stabbed Barney. He'd pushed that statue down the ladder and onto Michael's head, shattering his skull into pieces.

And then poor Jimmy had tried bashing that bathroom door down to get to Billy and whoever was helping him, only to get a toilet tank lid to the jaw.

Brutal. And if it wasn't his own people, he'd kind of respect it.

But they were his own people. Two of them dead. One of them, not far off.

He stood up and walked into the bathroom through the remains of the door. Over to the window. Looked down at the hole in the extension ceiling.

"They must've—they must've gone through there and then escaped through the garage," Kurt said, right by Ramiro's side now.

"And who was supposed to be watching the garage?" Ramiro asked.

Kurt lowered his head. Mumbled something.

"What was that?"

"Me," Kurt said. "It—it was me."

Ramiro knew it was Kurt already. Knew damned well it was. He'd seen the way Kurt ditched his post where he'd been asked to guard and went wandering into the house, giving Billy and the woman helping him a chance to get away. He saw how he'd bolted off down the street in pursuit of them, only to lose them both.

"So, you're telling me one of our children got away because you let him," Ramiro said.

Kurt couldn't even look him in the eye anymore. "I—I'm sorry. I fucked up."

Poor jawless Jimmy let out a loud, piercing gargle. A wail for help.

Ramiro felt his jaw tensing. He walked up to Kurt. Walked right up to him. He could feel the nervous heat radiating from his skin. "Two people are dead, Kurt. Two of our own. And Jimmy's not got long left."

"I know. I—I made a bad call. I'm sorry."

"Sorry won't bring them back," Ramiro said. Jimmy still wailing in the background now. Louder than before. "And the kid got away. The kid got away, and he got away with help. You realise how much of a fuck up this is?"

Kurt glanced up at him. He was crying. Shaking. Pathetic. "Please, Ramiro. I—"

Ramiro slapped him across the face. Hard. "You're pitiful. Look at you. Two people dead, and you're not crying for them. You're crying 'cause you fucked up and you feel sorry for yourself."

"That's not true."

Ramiro slapped him again. His anger building. He wanted to beat the fucker. He wanted to make him pay for this mistake.

'Cause someone had to be held responsible.

Ramiro grabbed him by the ear. Squeezed it hard.

"You're one mistake away from getting the Eustace treatment," Ramiro said.

"Please. Please."

"One mistake, Kurt. One fucking mistake."

Behind, Jimmy wailed even louder.

And Ramiro wasn't sure what it was that made him snap at that moment, but he just couldn't take it anymore.

"That fucker needs shutting up," he said.

He let go of Kurt's ear.

Pushed him out of the way.

And then he grabbed the bloodied toilet tank lid and walked over to Jimmy.

"I'm sorry, pal," he said. "But you really need putting out of your misery."

Jimmy's eyes widened.

His gargled scream grew louder than ever.

And then Ramiro slammed the lid against his skull.

And then again, just to be sure.

He dropped the lid. Stood there, gasping, shaking a little. Blood on his hands.

He looked down at the gory mess of Jimmy's caved-in head.

Then up at Kurt, who looked down at Jimmy with wide eyes, shivering.

"One more mistake, Kurt," Ramiro said. "One more fucking mistake."

And then he stepped over Jimmy's body and headed down the stairs.

It was time to track down Billy and that bitch who'd taken him away.

If they thought they were getting away that easily, they were very fucking mistaken.

CHAPTER FOURTEEN

It was already turning light when Aoife found an old, abandoned pub just off the canal, perfect for sheltering in for a while.

Okay, maybe not perfect. Didn't look in the best condition, as was to be expected. Looked like it might've been nice at some point, but the doors were all boarded up. A few of the windows were smashed. Didn't look like the kind of place anyone would be sheltering in or living in.

And that's why it was perfect for Aoife and Billy.

She looked down at him as he stood beside her. Quiet kid. A joy, in all truth. Didn't complain or whinge about anything. Just got on with things. She'd fully expect a kid in his position to be more cautious about things than he was. But he seemed so damned compliant.

And that saddened Aoife. Because again, a compliant kid like him must've been through all sorts of horrible shit at the hands of this Ramiro guy.

"This look okay to you?" Aoife asked.

Billy tilted his head like he was thinking about it. Then he nodded. "I guess."

"Not quite ticking all the boxes?"

"It looks kind of... scary."

"The scary places are always best. Means people are less likely to go looking in them. And besides. It's only for a few hours. Just get warm and grab some sleep. Then we... Well. Then we can figure out what we're going to do next."

She didn't want to think too much about that. Finding Kayleigh and Rex was her priority, obviously. But she had a young kid with her now. And he was her responsibility too, whether she liked it or not.

Making sure he stayed safe and away from Ramiro and his people. That was on her.

She thought about all the possibilities. One of the districts, like Sanctuary? An option. But a long journey.

And she couldn't stay somewhere like that herself. Not after...

Don't think about that.

There were other groups scattered around, of course. But there was a real lack of permanence to a solution like that. Every chance a kid like Billy could just fall into the same old shit again if that group was toppled, as seemed inevitable.

Because everything fell, these days.

At some point, everything fell.

She heard Billy's teeth chattering as a cold breeze battered the pair of them and realised they'd been stood outside for far too long.

"Come on. Let's get inside and get a fire lit. I can't wait to get out of this cold."

The pair of them walked over to the pub. Ended up climbing in through one of the broken windows. Once they were inside, Aoife looked around. Dark. Damp. A sour smell of alcohol that had gone off long ago. The stench of smoke sticking to the crusty carpets. Broken glass everywhere. Snapped pool cues and balls on the floor beside the table.

Over at the far side of the pub, a fireplace. A nice big fireplace.

"Just what we need," Aoife said.

They looked for stuff to burn. Aoife kept looking around to make sure nobody was in here, but she was pretty sure they were in the clear—apart from a few pigeons and mice, by the looks of things, but they weren't anything she couldn't handle.

Come to think of it, quite a few of those pigeons looked like they'd been bitten into. Probably just a fox or something.

But it made her feel a bit... well, iffy.

She grabbed old newspapers, filled with words about events that might have seemed significant at the time but took on a complete irrelevance now. She grabbed an old wooden kids' chair in the corner then searched for some matches, which she found behind the bar.

When the fireplace was full of fuel, she struck the match and set it alight.

"That's better," she said, the warmth hitting them right away. "Bit smoky, but better, huh?"

Billy looked into the flames, their orange glow flickering against his face. He looked comfortable but distant. Lost. She figured it made sense.

He was holding his hand tight. Looked like he had a little cut on there, which was bleeding.

"Your hand okay?"

He looked down at it like he hadn't even noticed. Then he looked at Aoife and nodded. "It'll be okay."

"I can... I can get a plaster or a bandage or something if you'd like?"

"It's okay," Billy said.

She didn't want to push him. So she nodded and gave him his space. Figured that's what he needed right now. She sat there beside him, in front of the fire. Stared into it as outside the sky grew slightly lighter, still doing nothing to illuminate the darkness of this pub, though.

"Get some rest if you can," Aoife said. "We've got a long few days ahead, and you're going to need your strength. We both are."

"Do you think things will ever be normal again?" Billy asked.

Aoife stared at him. The desperation and defeat in the poor kid's voice were crippling. To be asking a question like that all these years after the collapse.

Aoife wanted to be brutally honest. She never thought things would be normal again. Ever.

But for some strange reason, as much as she didn't like sugar-coating shit... she found herself half-smiling and nodding.

"Yeah," she said. "Yeah, I do."

Billy's eyes lit up. The flames flickered in them.

"Really?" he said.

Aoife looked at him, and for the first time in a long time, she felt hope.

"Get some sleep," she said. "We've got a long day ahead."

Billy opened his mouth like he was going to ask something else.

Then he just smiled at her. Nodded.

Rolled over on the hard floor and curled up into a little ball.

She looked at him and felt a tear roll down her face.

"Sleep well," he said.

She smiled. Swallowed a lump in her throat. "You too."

She leaned back against the carpet and stared up at the ceiling as the flames flickered at her feet.

* * *

SHE DIDN'T SEE the man standing at the window, watching.

CHAPTER FIFTEEN

Burning.

The sound of gunfire.

Ducking down and running as the static noise got louder and louder and louder…

"I'm sorry," Aoife gasped. "I'm sorry, I'm sorry, I'm…"

Standing on the outskirts of the place she'd called home.

Looking back at it. At the people in the streets. At people she used to know. People she used to love.

Looking at the smoke rising into the sky.

Wanting to go back there. Not wanting to leave anyone behind.

And then a bang, and then…

"Aoife!"

She opened her eyes and jolted forward.

She'd been asleep. The fire was still crackling away in front of her. She must've dozed off God knows how long ago. Her back ached. Her head was sore. And her chest was tight, too. Heart racing, pulse throbbing in her neck.

She was okay. Just a dream. That's all it was. Just a dream.

Dreams couldn't hurt anyone.

She looked over at where Billy lay, and her heart skipped a beat.

Billy was gone.

She stood up right away. Shaky. Squinted around the pub, into the darkness. Light shone in through the windows but barely illuminated this dusty, damp old place.

There was no sign of him downstairs.

Where the hell was he?

"Billy?"

She walked across the floor, both wanting to hurry and wanting to make as little noise as possible at the same time. Her head pulsated. Her chest grew tighter and tighter. Where the hell was he? Where the hell was he, and where had he gone?

"Billy?"

Her voice echoed around the pub.

Still nothing.

She felt dizzy and sick. A combination of emotions and thoughts flooded her mind.

Maybe this was a good thing.

Maybe this was for the best.

Maybe it was better he was gone because she didn't need that level of responsibility on her hands.

She couldn't look after anyone. She couldn't save anyone. She couldn't...

No.

Billy was her responsibility, whether she liked it or not.

She had to find him.

Wherever he was, he couldn't have gone far.

She looked at the floor. Looked for a sign of any footprints in the dust. Just anything that could give a clue away as to where he was, where he'd gone.

And then she saw it.

The blood.

Specks of blood on the carpet. Maybe from a while ago. But they looked newer. Fresh.

Only tiny. But enough to form a trail.

A trail that led right across the bar.

Right towards the narrow passageway past the toilets.

Right to the stairs.

Aoife stood at the foot of the stairs. Shaking. She had to go up there. She had to find him.

But at the same time... she dreaded what she might come across. What she might find. What kind of state he might be in.

He'd been through enough. The poor lad had been through enough.

And if something had happened on her watch.

If something had happened when she was supposed to be looking after him...

No.

Don't think that way.

Just get up those stairs and find him, you silly bitch.

She climbed the steps, tried to be slow and subtle about it, but it was no use. They were creaky as hell. Got to the point she stopped even trying to be subtle or careful because if there were somebody up here, they'd already know she was coming.

"Billy?" Aoife called.

No response.

She climbed further up. Saw three doors, all of them shut. Clenched her fists. She had to be ready. She had to go grab a weapon or something. She needed to be ready to fight if that's what it came to.

She went to head back downstairs when she saw movement.

It happened in a flash.

Sudden, and out of nowhere.

But unmistakable.

A woman.

And a dog.

"Kayleigh? Rex?"

She took a step down the stairs. Kept on descending. The sound from the static in her skull getting louder. The white noise getting more and more intense.

"Is that you?"

And then suddenly, just as she got to the bottom step, she heard a voice from above.

Billy's voice.

"I'm up here!"

She stopped. Froze. Her skin turned to ice.

She turned around. Looked back up those stairs.

"Billy?"

"It's okay," he said. "I'm upstairs."

She stood there. Shaking. This wasn't right. None of it felt right. First, Kayleigh and Rex. And now Billy, upstairs.

The static getting louder.

Keep your shit together, Aoife. Pull it the fuck together...

She looked back. Squinted into the fire-lit darkness of the pub.

No sign of Kayleigh or Rex.

"Fuck it," she said.

She climbed the stairs. Got to the top.

"Which room you in, Billy?"

No response.

"Billy," she said, walking towards the first door on the left. "This... this isn't a game. Where the hell are..."

She opened that first door and stopped right away.

Billy was sitting at a table. There was a board game in front of him. Monopoly, by the looks of things.

And sitting opposite him, there was a thin, pale, bearded man with a beaming smile across his face.

And a knife right in front of him, on the table.

"But it *is* a game, love," he said. "It *is* a game. Do you care to join us?"

CHAPTER SIXTEEN

"Come on, dear. Take a seat. And don't be alarmed. We just wanted to get the game set up for when you woke, didn't we, little bear? Come, come. We're all ready now. Take a seat. Don't keep the game-master waiting!"

Aoife stood in the doorway to this room at the back of the pub. Looked like it'd been a child's room once upon a time, with board games stacked up in the corner, gathering dust. A single bed with Spiderman on the covers, all dirty and mouldy. Windows boarded up with drawings across the wood. Children's drawings.

And the closer Aoife looked, the more she noticed the skeletal remains on top of the bed.

The remains of a child.

"Come on," the man said, waving her along to the little table in the middle of the room, which the Monopoly board game sat atop. He was a thin guy with a long beard, and he had these manic eyes. Reeked of sweat, too. And was that a hint of alcohol in the air? She wasn't sure. Could just be 'cause it was a pub.

But he was waving at her to join. Smiling.

Knife sitting on the table.

One thing was for sure. This man wasn't right in the head.

Aoife looked past him, over at Billy. She could see he was afraid, the scene before her barely illuminated by the soft candlelight. She could see the fear in his bloodshot eyes.

But at the same time, she knew there was no other way out of this than by being patient. By being careful.

She'd dealt with people like this plenty of times since the world collapsed. The best thing? To go along with their plan until you found yourself a chance to make a break for it.

'Cause they weren't evil or nasty or even had any bad intentions. They were just… sad. Afraid. Lost.

They just needed something.

Connection.

Aoife had to give this man connection.

And then she had to get her and Billy the hell out of here.

"Sit," the man said. "Please. Oh. I… How rude of me not to introduce myself. I'm Gordon. This—this here is my son, my little Bear."

Aoife realised now that he was referring to Billy as Bear as a name itself, not a pet name.

And that he actually thought Billy was his son.

"Nice to meet you, Gordon. I'm Aoife."

And then she nodded at Billy. Half-smiled. Tried to be as calm and reassuring as possible. "Bear. Nice to meet you too."

"Good," Gordon said, smiling, laughing, looking between the pair of them like he couldn't quite believe this connection was taking place before his eyes. "Now—now come on. Sit yourself down. We've been waiting for so long to play, me and Bear. So, so long. Years! Haven't we, Bear?"

Billy nodded.

"I said, haven't we, Bear?"

"Yes," Billy said.

"No!" Gordon shouted. Then he slammed a fist down on the table before him. "Not you. The… the other. My other Bear."

Aoife's mouth went dry. That snap, that show of temper. This was one very disturbed individual. And this might not be as easy to get out of as Aoife had hoped.

"Sit," Gordon said. A lot calmer now. Smiling and laughing a little nervously like he worried Aoife had seen him for who he truly was.

Aoife smiled at him. "Sure. I'm coming."

She walked over to the table. Kept her eyes on the knife.

She was going to grab it at some point.

And she was going to get Billy out of here.

"Now," Gordon said, his voice all shaky. "I... You know, I can't remember the rules. Can you remember the rules?"

He looked right at Aoife.

"I..."

"Maybe we can just—just talk instead. Or play another game. A guessing game!"

"Whatever you'd like to play, Gordon," Aoife said.

She looked at Billy.

Then back at Gordon again, who was rocking back and forth on his chair, getting more and more worked up.

"I'll go first. Guess... guess how long I've been in here. In here, eating the rats. Eating the pigeons. And they make my stomach so bad. They make it hurt so, so, so bad."

Aoife thought back to the pigeons she'd found downstairs, the toothmarks in them, and she felt a bit sick.

The sooner she got hold of that knife, the better.

"Anyway," Gordon said. "Guess!"

"Erm... a year?" Aoife asked.

Gordon nodded. He looked like he was thinking it through. "A year. Has it been a year? Is that how long me and my Bear have been in here? Is that right, Bear?"

Billy stayed quiet this time. Very still. Especially after last time.

"Bear?"

He looked around at Billy.

"Sorry," Billy said. "I... I don't know."

"Come here," Gordon said.

"What?"

"Come here and sit on Daddy's knee."

Aoife felt herself tense up. Saw Billy go even stiffer, too, like a statue.

"Come on, Bear," Gordon said. Sadness to his voice. "Come sit on Daddy's knee."

Billy looked over at Aoife with wide eyes.

With total fear.

And she saw a million things in Billy's gaze.

She saw the flashbacks to things he'd obviously already been through.

The horror, after thinking he'd got away. After thinking this was over.

"Come on," Gordon said. He sounded like he was crying now.

Aoife held her breath. Stared at Billy. Waited for whatever happened next.

And then she watched as Billy climbed off his chair, walked over to Gordon, and sat on his knee.

Gordon laughed. Tears rolled down his face as he held Billy on his knee, as he hugged him, buried his face into Billy's neck. "Good boy. My good, good boy. We're okay. We'll be okay. We're family. And I'm never letting you go again. Never."

Aoife saw Gordon's eyes close.

Saw him so focused on Billy, lost in a trance.

She went to reach for the knife when she suddenly heard something downstairs.

A knock.

"Anyone in there?" a man shouted.

Gordon opened his eyes.

Frowned.

"Visitors?" he said. "I wasn't expecting..."

And then he saw Aoife's hand hovering over the knife.

CHAPTER SEVENTEEN

"Hello? Anyone home?"

Aoife heard the voice downstairs. The knock on the door. Someone was here.

But it was Gordon she was looking at most.

She had her hand over the knife on the little Monopoly table in front of her. Held it there. It looked like it was hovering, suspended in time. She wanted to move her hand away, to convince Gordon she wasn't making a break for it.

But at the same time, she wanted to grab it. Wanted to point it at Gordon and get him the fuck away from Billy, who sat on his knee, Gordon's thin, spindly fingers wrapped around him.

But Gordon was looking right at her with wide eyes. With terror on his face. Holding Billy tighter, now.

"You brought them here," he said.

Aoife shook her head. Downstairs, she heard more banging and the sound of someone entering the house. "Gordon, you need to listen to me—"

"You brought them here to take my Bear away! But no! I won't let you! I won't let you take him away!"

"Bear's already gone, Gordon."

Gordon shook his head. Squeezed his crying eyes shut. "No!"

"He's gone," Aoife said. Fully realising this could be a very dangerous and costly change of tack. "He's gone, and that boy on your lap there is called Billy. Not Bear."

"No!" Gordon shouted. Squeezing Billy closer. "He's—he's my boy! He's my boy!"

"Gordon," Aoife said. Standing up. Not holding the knife. She didn't want to grab it. Didn't want to threaten this man any more. "You need to listen to me. There's people after Billy. Very dangerous people who want to do horrible things to him. Who wish him harm. I'm... I'm worried they might be here already. If you don't let us leave, they'll kill us, and they'll take Billy away, and they'll do even worse things to him."

Footsteps on the stairs.

They were coming.

"You there, Billy Bob?" a voice said.

Shit. It was them.

"Gordon," Aoife said, trying to turn her attention from the voices and focus solely on Gordon and Billy. "Please. I'm begging you. I'm sorry for what you've been through. I'm sorry for what you've lost. For what happened to your boy. I'm more sorry than you could ever realise. But right now isn't the time for this, Gordon. We're all in trouble. Big trouble. Unless we get out of here. Right this second."

He looked into Aoife's eyes with tears streaming down his face. And for a moment, just for a second, she thought she saw a flicker of connection there. A glimmer of understanding.

"Please, Gordon," she said. "Please."

He opened his mouth like he was going to say something.

"My Bear," he said. "People... people hurt him. I couldn't feed him. I had to... I had to let people... I'm sorry. I'm so sorry."

She didn't want to know what Gordon was implying. But she'd made progress. The smallest of progress but progress all the same.

"Please, Gordon. Put Billy down. We need to get out of here. We need to get out of this room. Right now."

Gordon looked down at Billy. Like he didn't recognise him. Like he was waking up.

And then he loosened his grip on him.

"Good," Aoife said. "Good."

He started to loosen his grip and let Billy go when the door to this room suddenly slammed open.

Aoife looked around.

In the doorway, she saw a man. Dark, curly hair. Dressed in black.

Smile on his face.

There were two other men right behind him.

"Hello, Billy," the man said. "You don't have to worry anymore, kid."

CHAPTER EIGHTEEN

"You don't have to worry anymore, kid. It's me. Ol' Uncle Ramiro. Don't look so sheepish. We know each other well. Real well, right?"

That smirk across his face. The way he spoke with such arrogance. Such confidence. It made Aoife's blood boil.

And the fact that this was him. This was Ramiro. This was the man who had kidnapped Billy. Who had taken him away from safety. Who'd forced him through unthinkable hell.

He was here. Right here in the door of this room. Knife in hand. Two other men by his side.

"What's up, kiddo?" Ramiro asked. "You look scared. There's no need to be scared. I mean. You're a bad lad for running off. A real bad lad. But you knew that. You knew what the risks were. And, hell. I can't blame you for wanting to fly the nest. You're getting to that age. Only natural to be curious about the world around you, huh? But it's okay. We're here now. And we're gonna be okay. We're gonna get you out of here, and everything's gonna be okay."

He hadn't even looked at Aoife or Gordon yet. Just stared at

Billy like he was trying to get through to him, trying to manipulate him somehow.

Billy stood in front of Gordon, who still held on to him, but only loosely now.

"Not my Bear," Gordon said. "Not... not my Bear."

Ramiro looked up at Gordon. Scanned him, head to toe, like he was disgusted by the sight of him. "What was that, sir? You been looking after my lad for me? Well, I'm here for him now. You don't have to worry about looking after him anymore."

He looked around the room, then. Around the darkness, clearly taking in his surroundings. The dirt. The grime.

And the skeletal remains lying on the bed at the far side of the room.

"Nice place you got here," he said. "Now, come on, Billy. We'd best be getting you back home, hadn't we? Don't want to make things any worse for yourself. Don't want to end up in even bigger trouble. Right?"

Billy shook his head. And then he started walking, started trying to get back to Ramiro. Like a moth to a flame. Knowing just how much he would be burned but fearing anything other than the familiarity.

And worrying about the consequences of *not* going back to Ramiro.

She saw Gordon loosening his grip on Billy, muttering under his breath. "Not Bear. Billy. Not Bear."

Fucking hell. The one moment Aoife actually wanted Gordon to be protective, he looked like he was seeing sense. Fearing for his own life and realising Billy wasn't the son he was trying to protect.

Bad timing, once again.

Ramiro smiled. Laughed a little. "That's right. You know what's good for you. And I appreciate it, kiddo. I respect it. I know this can't be easy. But you're doing the right thing. You're..."

Aoife lunged for Billy. Grabbed his arm and dragged him back, which made him whimper a little.

And it was then that Ramiro finally looked at her. Finally acknowledged her. Finally paid her any kind of attention.

He looked at her, and for a moment, just a split second, his smile dropped.

And then it came back, even wider than before.

Like he recognised her.

"Well," he said. "I didn't see you standing there in the dark. You must be the woman who killed my friends. How rude of me not to introduce myself. Ramiro. And you are?"

"It doesn't matter who I am," Aoife said, tightening her grip around Billy's arm. "The things you've done to this kid. The things you've put him through... It's over."

Ramiro smirked. Shrugged. "Hear that, boys? It's over, apparently."

His friends laughed. Shook their heads.

"How about we deal with this like responsible adults, hmm? How about we ask the kid what he wants?"

"He's just a kid," Aoife said, her voice shaking. "A kid you've manipulated. A kid you've—"

"What is it you want, Billy? You want to come back home with us? Where you're warm, and you're safe, and you'll be fed? Or you want to go running into the wilds with this one?"

Billy looked up at Aoife. His eyes were wide. He looked lost. Confused. Practically unrecognisable. Since Ramiro had got here, he had transformed quickly from a hardened kid—scared and compliant but hardened—to someone who looked truly lost.

"Billy," Aoife said. "You don't want this. He doesn't want this."

"Billy," Ramiro said. A little sterner. "You know what's right for you. And you know damn well what'll happen if you don't. You know what's happened before when kids have gone running. They've never *stayed* running. And the longer they've run, the more they've tried to get away... You know how it ends, Billy."

Billy lowered his head. He started shaking, quite violently, in Aoife's grasp.

"I'm not promising you the world," Aoife said. "But I'm promising you better than things are with him. You know it's worth it, Billy. You know that. Deep down."

She saw him turn to her. Look right up at her, into her eyes.

And then he lowered his head, and he nodded.

"I just... I just want to go back," he said.

Ramiro smiled. "Hear that? He wants to come back. Kid's made a decision."

Aoife's stomach sank. "You've brainwashed him. Manipulated him—"

"He's made a decision. He wants to come back. So you'd better respect that, lady. And while we're here... for what you did to my people. To my friends... That shit doesn't go unpunished."

Ramiro took a step further into the room. His two friends close beside him.

"So hand him over. Hand him over and then accept responsibility for what you've done. Don't make this harder on yourself. On either of you."

Aoife looked at Billy. Kept tight hold of his hand.

And then she looked at Ramiro, and then at Gordon, who stood there, still muttering under his breath.

"Please," Billy cried. Clearly terrified. "Please."

She took a deep breath.

Swallowed a lump in her throat.

And then she loosened her grip on Billy's arm.

CHAPTER NINETEEN

oife loosened her grip on Billy's shaking arm, and she felt terrible about what she was going to do next.

She looked at Gordon. Still caught in that frenzied state. Still barely clutching on to reality. And as bad as she felt for him because he was clearly just a lost and tortured soul, she knew she had to use him if she was going to get out of this mess.

She loosened her grip on Billy's arm some more.

Saw Ramiro and his men walking towards her as if in slow motion.

And then she tightened her grip on Billy's arm again.

"Gordon, these men are the ones who killed Bear."

Gordon looked at her. Frowned. "What?" More lucid, now. More present.

"These men killed Bear. They killed your son. They're the ones who killed him."

Ramiro frowned. Looked from Aoife to Gordon. "I don't know what—"

"You killed him," Gordon said.

He stepped towards Ramiro. Towards the two men beside him.

"You killed him. You killed Bear. It—it was you."

Aoife held on to Billy, and she knew she had a really small window to act here.

But that's exactly what she had to do.

"Don't worry, Billy," she said. "We've got this."

And then, before she could change her mind, she dragged him back.

Over towards that bed.

Over to the window.

Prayed it was unlocked. Prayed she could open it.

Behind her, she heard commotion. Shouting.

"You killed him!" Gordon shouted. Throwing himself at Ramiro. Frenzied and primitive. "You killed Bear!"

She felt bad for him. The distraction she'd needed. And that's exactly how she'd treated him.

But she couldn't afford to feel bad about anything right now.

She clambered over the remains of Bear's skeleton. Grabbed the handle of the window and turned it.

Please be open; please be open, please...

The handle didn't budge.

"Fuck," Aoife said.

She looked around for a key. Saw one on the window ledge, right there. What fucking use was that?

She grabbed it and dropped it with her shaking fingers.

Then she heard punching and spluttering.

She looked back. Gordon was being stabbed by Ramiro.

But he was still standing his ground.

He was still fighting.

And he was still holding them back.

She turned, grabbed the key, and then she stuck it in the window lock.

"Come on," she said. "Come on..."

She turned it.

Opened the handle, which was stiff and felt like it might just snap away.

And then she pushed the window open and felt a sudden icy burst of wind.

"Through here, Billy. Now."

She saw him staring. Wide-eyed. Like he was unsure about this. Couldn't blame him. He'd already jumped out of one window in the last few hours after all, and that hadn't exactly gone well.

She heard less resistance behind. Less commotion and fight.

Looked back.

Gordon was slumped on the floor now.

Ramiro clambered over him, getting back to his feet.

Running towards them.

"Now," Aoife said. "Now!"

She turned, pushed the window further open, and then she looked down at the drop.

It wasn't good. Wasn't good at all.

But it was this, or it was the alternative.

And the alternative wasn't something she wanted to entertain.

She grabbed Billy. Held him tight. Heard him crying. Felt him shaking.

"It's okay," she said. "I've got you. We've got this."

She held on to him and really didn't know how this was going to go.

But she knew that the alternative was far, far worse.

For both of them.

She swallowed a lump in her throat and went to step off the window ledge.

"Don't."

She looked around.

Ramiro stood there. For the first time since seeing him, Aoife thought he actually looked fearful.

"You don't want to do this," he said. "You'll never make it. Do this, and you know exactly what'll happen. There's still a chance to make this easier on both of you. But if you step out this window... I can't promise anything."

She felt a twinge of nerves. Of trepidation.

Looked back out of the window and at the drop below.

"I can only promise one thing, actually," Ramiro said.

Aoife looked back at him.

He smiled. "It will be painful. For both of you."

She stood there. Totally still. Winter winds battering against her.

And then she took a deep breath of that bitter, cold air and did the only thing she could do.

She held on to Billy, and she stepped out of the window, out into the darkness.

CHAPTER TWENTY

Aoife opened her eyes.

It was bright. Really bright. Burning sun shining down on her. Which was weird, 'cause she was pretty sure it was the middle of winter, but what the hell.

She looked around. Couldn't quite tell where she was. Just sort of lying here in a cloud of... brightness. That's the only way she could describe it.

It was strange, though. She couldn't really remember what'd led her here or how she'd ended up here. A vague sense of discontent maybe, somewhere in the back of her mind.

She tried to find that trepidation. Tried to locate it. Tried to unearth her memories, which felt buried and yet so close to the surface.

And then she felt something sloppy licking her face.

She squeezed her eyes shut, shook her head, and then backed off when she realised it was Rex.

"Rex," she said. "Silly boy. What're you doing here?"

He stood there, right before her. Wagging his little docked tail. She felt so happy to see him. She wasn't sure why she was crying at the same time.

Because somewhere in her mind, she'd told herself she would never see him again.

"I've missed you," she said. Sensing she'd not seen him for a long time. Did he have a light brown patch above his left eye or his right? Was he always this chunky? "I've missed you so much."

She ruffled his fur, soaked in the closeness, the connection. The warmth. It felt like a long time since she'd had that. Since she'd experienced it first-hand.

She tried to sink into this dream as much as she could when she heard footsteps approaching.

She turned around, squinted into that bright light above, and saw Kayleigh standing there.

She had her hands on her hips. A smile on her face. And Aoife couldn't really make out her features, weirdly. It was like, whenever she focused on one thing, she disappeared into a haze. The only way to look at her was loosely. Softly. Without looking at her too closely.

"Kayleigh," she said.

"Surprised to see me?" she asked.

Aoife nodded. Smiled. She tried to sit up, but it was like she was stuck here. Pinned to the ground, somehow. "I... I don't know. You were in the house, and then you just..."

"Left," Kayleigh said. "Right after you'd seen someone in the street. Ain't that a coincidence?"

Aoife didn't know what she meant. Didn't know what she was talking about.

Well. Maybe there was a part of her that got it. A part of her that understood. But that part was buried deep inside. And it was somewhere she didn't want to go.

"What... what is this place?"

Kayleigh shrugged. "This place is whatever you want it to be. But there's one thing for sure."

Aoife tensed up because she feared she knew exactly what Kayleigh would say.

"Don't go there," Aoife said.

"But eventually, you're going to *have* to go there. Because it's holding you back. It's stopping you moving forward."

"I'll move forward when I'm ready to."

"It's been eighteen months, Aoife. Eighteen months. And you think things are getting better? Really?"

Aoife closed her eyes, but she couldn't hide from Kayleigh. From Rex. Or from the brightness.

She felt Kayleigh's hand on her face. Soft. Gentle.

Looked up and saw her eyes now. Tearful but bright. Hopeful. Optimistic.

"You know you have to give up searching for me. You know you have to give up searching for Rex."

"No," Aoife said.

"And you know you have to give up searching for us because—"

"No!" Aoife shouted.

Right at that moment, she heard it. The explosion of white noise. Of gunfire.

Running away. Looking back at Sanctuary and knowing that everything had changed. That everything was different, all over again.

She opened her eyes, and this time, Kayleigh was hazy and blurry, even more so than before. Rex was just out of focus, too. And she wanted them to come back. Wanted them to come back so dearly.

"Don't lose sight of what's most important," Kayleigh said.

"And what's that?"

Kayleigh just smiled. "That's for you to figure out. Deep inside."

She disappeared, then. Disappeared into the brightness, which exploded. Into the warm light that surrounded Aoife, taking Rex away with her.

And then she coughed and opened her eyes.

She was outside. In the cold. Lying on her back. She was in pain. A lot of pain.

She remembered, then.

Jumping out of the window with Billy.

She had a horrible sense that something was wrong. That Billy had been taken. That he was gone.

But then she felt him.

Felt his warmth moving in her arms.

"You're okay," she said, wincing as she tried to get to her feet. "You're..."

That's when she saw he was bleeding badly from his head.

And his ankle was twisted. Looked like he was struggling to stand on it.

She lifted him. Held him close. "It's okay. We'll get out of this. Come on. We've got to..."

That's when she heard the footsteps, right around the side of the house.

They were coming.

Ramiro was coming.

CHAPTER TWENTY-ONE

Aoife heard the footsteps racing down the path at the side of the house, and she knew she had to get away. Fast.

She held on to Billy. Carried him over her shoulder. He was light as a feather. Bleeding from his head, and his ankle looked a little twisted, but he seemed okay otherwise.

Which was a relief, considering the pair of them had jumped out of a window. Big relief that she felt okay, too. At least she was still strong enough to be able to carry him.

"Come on," she said, turning and moving as quickly towards the back fence as she could. Her legs felt sore and achy. It hurt to put pressure on her feet. But mostly, she was okay. Okay enough to be able to stand. To be able to run—slowly, but anything was better than nothing.

She ran across the garden towards the fence. Behind, she could hear those footsteps getting closer. Time was running out. And she didn't really fancy her chances of climbing this fence in the first place.

But, shit. She had to keep going. She couldn't just stand here and give up.

She had to try.

She reached the fence at the bottom of the garden and realised she would have to do something she didn't want to do.

She was going to have to let go of Billy.

Let him climb the fence and drop to the other side.

And then she was going to have to climb it herself.

He was small for his age, so he wouldn't be able to climb it on his own. He needed a hand.

"Billy, there's only one way we can do this. I'm... I'm going to have to help you over. You're going to have to drop to the other side. And when we get over there... well. We'll figure that out as we go."

Billy nodded. Crying but nodding. Realising the urgency of this situation.

"I'm sorry," Aoife said. "For putting us both in danger. But... but I'm not going to let you go back with that savage. And I'm not going to let anything happen to you either. We're going to get out of this. I promise. Okay?"

He looked at her. A little less trust in his eyes than before.

And then he looked back over to the house.

"Don't look back," Aoife said. "We need to go. Now."

She lifted Billy up. Lifted him high enough to reach for the top of the fence.

He grabbed onto it. Pulled himself up.

"Good," she said. "Drop down to the other side. I'll be with you in no time. I promise."

He looked down at her. A stare that felt like it lasted forever.

"Go," she said, grabbing the top of the fence herself. "Now!"

She watched him drop down to the other side.

Heard a thud as he landed in the next garden.

Pulled herself up and heard footsteps right behind.

"Don't even think about it."

She reached the top of the fence. Turned around.

Ramiro stood there. Three people surrounding him.

None of them slowing down.

Ramiro had a look on his face. Something between anger and enjoyment. Like he was getting something from this. Enjoying the hunt.

"You're just making this worse for yourself," Ramiro said. "You're making it worse for Billy."

"I'm making nothing worse for either of us," Aoife said. "Because we're leaving here. And we won't have to worry about you anymore. Neither of us will."

Ramiro narrowed his eyes. She saw him open his mouth, go to say something else.

And before she could hear it, she dropped down.

Landed in the tall grass.

Looked around.

"Billy?"

Her stomach sank.

Billy was nowhere to be seen.

She heard Ramiro and his people running across the grass. They'd be here in no time. She couldn't hang around. She had to get moving.

There was a track.

A track in the tall grass leading to the other side of the garden.

To the path at the side of the house, which led out onto the road.

Billy must've gone that way. He must've made a break for it.

She started to run down it when she heard a whistle, to her left.

Looked around and saw Billy's head poking out of an old, rotting wooden shed.

"Billy," Aoife said.

"Run along the grass," Billy said. "Make it look like you've gone through the garden. Then come back this way. Round the path."

Her eyes lit up.

Clever little bugger.

"Quick!"

She ran across the garden.

Heard Ramiro's people slam against the fence.

She turned and ran down the path, almost slipping on the patio.

Heard more banging against that fence.

They were coming.

Time was running out.

She ran down the uneven concrete path at the side of the garden, and then she threw herself towards that shed.

Landed right in front of Billy.

Pulled him back and lay inside it, right beside him.

She stayed still. Very still. Held on to Billy, whose teeth chattered right beside her.

She watched as Ramiro landed in the garden. As the rest of his people landed beside him.

"It's okay," she whispered. "Everything's going to be okay."

She kept a tight hold of him as Ramiro looked around.

As he looked over at the shed, looking right at her for one nervous second.

And then he looked away again and started running through the garden, along the track in the grass.

Aoife watched them all run through the grass. Watched them disappear down the path at the side of the house.

"Ssh," she said to Billy, stroking his hair. "It'll be okay. Everything'll be okay."

She wasn't sure how long she lay there in this shed, Billy by her side, stroking him, trying to reassure him.

But she knew they were okay.

For now, they were okay.

For now, they were safe.

CHAPTER TWENTY-TWO

Aoife wasn't sure how long she'd been walking with Billy when he finally asked her the question that changed everything.

"Aren't you going to go find your friend again?"

She stopped walking. She was on an old main road leading right through to a town centre. Looked like it had been busy once. Loads of cars blocking the streets. The stranded cars were just as much a part of the scenery as trees were now. And they'd been there that long that foliage grew over them. Nature making its mark on a world that humanity had been so arrogant to assume was theirs for so long.

In the end, nature always prevailed.

But it was Billy's question that stopped her in her tracks. They'd been walking for a while. Not really speaking. Aoife didn't know what there was to say. And there were things she didn't want to talk about, either. What she'd done to Gordon. Throwing him in the way of her and Billy like that, using him as a tool to help their escape.

And dragging Billy off when he'd chosen to stay with Ramiro.

She knew it was in his best interests. But at the end of the day, she'd still denied the boy a choice, in a sense.

But no. She couldn't feel guilty about that. Ramiro was a monster, and Billy was far better off without him.

And yet... did Ramiro have a point?

What sort of life was he going to live with Aoife?

Where was she going to take him?

Where were they going to go?

But again, that question lingered in her mind.

Aren't you going to go find your friend again?

She didn't know how to answer that question. Because, of course, she wanted to find Kayleigh again. And, of course, she wanted to find Rex again.

But...

"You know you have to give up searching for me. You know you have to give up searching for Rex."

Kayleigh's words, in that weird state of consciousness after she'd thrown herself out the window.

"You have to give up searching for me because..."

The white noise in her skull.

So noisy it was painful.

"Better if we just keep walking, for now," Aoife said.

"But what if Ramiro finds her?"

"What?"

"What if Ramiro finds your friend? And your dog? What if something bad happens to them, and they don't know—"

"Look, I don't think Ramiro's going to find them, okay? And if he does, I don't think he'll be all that interested in them."

Billy lowered his head. She felt a bit guilty in all truth for being so snappy. But Billy was getting too close to the truth for comfort.

He was getting too close to making her admit something she really, really didn't want to.

"That man. In the house. The one who thought I was Bear. That was… that was sad. What happened."

Aoife felt her body tensing up. She really didn't need Billy making her feel guilty about that. She felt guilty enough about it as it was. Didn't need an extra layer of guilt on top of it.

"It's a shame," Aoife said. "But if we hadn't done that, we wouldn't have got away."

"You should… you should have just let me go."

"What?"

"You should have let me go with Ramiro. If he catches us now, it'll be bad. Really bad. If you'd let me go back… it wouldn't be good, but it would be better than it will be. You could have run away. You didn't… you didn't have to help me."

She heard him saying these things, not quite looking her in the eye, and again, she felt so sad and guilty for being so snappy. 'Cause this kid was actually admitting he'd sacrifice his own comfort for her. He felt bad about what happened to Gordon. Bad about Aoife ending up having to look after him.

She felt so, so sorry for him.

"Hey," Aoife said. "Look at me."

Billy looked up at her.

She crouched down. Put her hands on his shoulders. "You're not a burden, okay? I'm helping you because I want to help you. And not just that. I… I'm actually rather enjoying your company, dare I admit it."

Billy smiled. "You're not as mean as I thought you were."

"You thought I was mean?"

"When we first met. I thought… I don't know. You seem like you're hurting. Like you're… like you're lost. But maybe you just need a friend."

Aoife heard Billy's words, and she felt herself welling up. He might look small, but he was fourteen, and fourteen was old enough to make mature observations like that.

"You need a friend," he said. "Don't you?"

When he said those words, she felt an arrow of sadness right to her chest.

Sudden. Sharp. Painful and hot.

The gun.

The power source.

Pulling the trigger and the sound of static and...

"I've got you," Aoife said. "And wherever... wherever my friends are out there, they'll be okay. They'll find a way. Kayleigh... Kayleigh's not keen on dogs, but she's good with Rex. She'll be good with him. She'll look after him."

She turned away. Started walking again, down the road.

"I heard you," Billy said.

Aoife stopped. Turned around. "What?"

He looked up at her with these big, knowing eyes, and she feared what was coming already.

He twiddled with his hands. "When... when I was in the attic. I heard you. Talking."

Static.

White noise.

Louder and louder and—

"You were talking with... with two voices. Like you were speaking to someone. But there was only you."

He said those words, and Aoife wanted to shake her head.

She wanted to fight it.

She wanted to resist it.

"Let's—let's not talk about this, Billy. Please."

But he didn't look like he was stopping.

"I heard you say her name. Kayleigh. And then I heard you say *your* name. In the same voice."

She shook her head. Well, her entire *body* shook. She couldn't fight it. She couldn't run from it. She couldn't deny it. Not anymore.

"You're... you're the same person," Billy said. "Kayleigh... Kayleigh isn't real. She isn't real. Is she?"

He said those words, and she wanted to fight.

She wanted to resist.

But she knew she couldn't run anymore.

She squeezed her eyes shut, and as much as she didn't want to admit it, as much as she didn't want to face it, she said the words she'd never expected to say.

"She was real," Aoife said, tears streaming down her face. "Both of them *were* real... once."

And then a weight lifted from her shoulders, and darkness surrounded her.

CHAPTER TWENTY-THREE

She was back at the power source again.

It was dark. Dark, but for those torchlights, all beaming towards her. Her hand was shaky, sweaty. She felt so nervous. So exhausted.

And yet she knew deep down exactly what she had to do.

Even if it went against every logical instinct in her body.

"Put the pistol down," Yuri said. Holding that gun to Kayleigh's head. "Put it down, and it ends. Put it down, and you live. Both of you live."

She looked at Kayleigh. Looked into her eyes. Saw the way she stared at her. The way she nodded.

And as much as Aoife didn't want to lose her, she knew what that nod meant.

She knew exactly what Kayleigh would be saying to her right now if she could speak.

This is bigger than me. It's bigger than both of us.

She took a deep breath, and she knew there was only one thing she could do.

She knew this was bigger than the pair of them.

This wasn't just for her community.

This was for the very future of this country.

"There's only one thing more important than power," Aoife said.

Yuri frowned. "And what's that?"

Aoife lifted her pistol.

"Connection," she said.

She kept her focus steady on the power source.

Held her breath.

Closed her eyes.

And she pulled the trigger.

A BLAST.

An explosion of static.

A bang, so loud that the sheer sound of it knocked her off her feet and sent her flying across the room.

She hit her head against a wall. Her ears rang. She couldn't hear anything but that static.

When she looked around, blinking, trying to see, she saw burning.

Flames rising from the power source.

Spreading rapidly around this dark tomb.

Smoke rising into the air.

Yuri's people, some of them holding their ground, some of them scattered around the room. Some of them lying dead on the floor.

And some of them running away. Trying to make a break from this burning room before it became their grave.

She squinted around the room as the flickering orange light from the flames grew brighter. Searched for Yuri. For Kayleigh. She had to get to her. She had to get to her, and she had to get to Rex, and then they had to get out of here.

She scrambled to her feet. Limped across the floor, over towards that exit. The people here were so caught up and distracted by the blast that they didn't seem to see Aoife gliding by. It's like she was irrelevant to them now. What mattered more was survival.

And what mattered more was the fact that she'd just pulled the trigger and ended the very thing that made them so powerful.

She reached the doorway leading back out towards the ladder. So dark out there. Still no sign of Kayleigh or Yuri.

She kept low and crept down this dark corridor. People ran past her, pushed by her. It was so dark, and the torchlights were waving everywhere that it gave her another sense of security. It was dangerous; she knew it was. But she knew where she was going. She knew the way out of here far better than the rest of them here. She knew these labyrinth passageways.

But she didn't know where Kayleigh was.

She ran down the corridor. She could feel the flames getting hotter behind her. She could see the orange glow creeping up around the corridor like it was chasing her. She had to keep on going. Couldn't look back. Couldn't stop. Not for anything or anyone.

She took a right. Almost tumbled over a man crawling along. It took her a few glances to realise he was missing a leg.

She felt for him. Felt for anyone in pain.

But at the same time... he was one of Yuri's people.

And even if he wasn't, she didn't have the time to save anyone right now.

Anyone but Kayleigh and Rex.

She ran down the corridor. Slammed into a door. Fuck. Must've taken a wrong turn somewhere.

She turned and tried to get her bearings. But all she could see was that orange glow creeping closer. Smoke thickening, making her splutter. She could hear more people now, too. Crying through the static. Screaming.

She held on to the wall to feel for the turn. It went on longer than she expected. And for a second, she wondered if she'd got completely lost. Heading right back towards that orange glow and towards that smoke…

But then she felt the turn in the wall, and she knew she was on the right track again.

You've got this. You can do this. You can fucking make this.

She ran down the dark corridor. Still no sign of Kayleigh anywhere. Where the hell was she? Yuri couldn't have got this far, surely.

She reached the ladder. The way out. Looked back. She'd have to go back. She'd have to search for her. She'd have to—

Another bang.

Flames filling the corridor.

Screaming.

She looked back. She knew she was screwed now. The corridor was blocked. There was no way out. No way back.

But she couldn't leave Kayleigh behind.

She went to head back inside the maze of corridors when suddenly, she saw her.

She was limping along. Leaning against the wall. Yuri was right there, too, right by her side.

"Kayleigh," Aoife said.

Kayleigh stared up at her. Sweat and blood all over her face. Clutching her ribs. "Go, Aoife."

Aoife shook her head. "I'm not leaving you—"

"Go!"

But Aoife wasn't listening.

She ran towards Kayleigh.

That's when she felt another hot blast.

An explosion, right in front of her, sending her flying through the air.

Slamming back against the ladders.

She crouched there. Stared at the flames.

"Kayleigh!"

Her voice echoed around the corridor.

The corridor that was growing hotter and hotter like a furnace.

Tears and smoke filled her eyes. She wanted to go back there. She wanted to get to her. She didn't want to walk away.

But there was no way she was getting through this wall of flames.

"I'm sorry," she said. "I'm so sorry."

She closed her burning eyes as screaming filled the corridors.

Then she grabbed the hot metal steps of the ladder and hauled herself up.

She didn't look back until she reached the outskirts of Sanctuary.

Looked back at the rising smoke.

At the flames.

And then she turned around and didn't look back again.

CHAPTER TWENTY-FOUR

Aoife sat back against the abandoned Land Rover in the middle of the road and couldn't quite believe she'd finally admitted what she'd just admitted.

It was raining a little. Making the snow all brown and slushy. Didn't feel as cold as usual right now. But maybe that was just 'cause Aoife was so worked up with what she'd just admitted.

The truth about Kayleigh.

The truth about what happened at Sanctuary, eighteen months ago.

Not only had she admitted it to Billy, but she'd admitted it to herself, too.

She glanced around at Billy. Saw him sitting there beside her, rubbing his hands together. She felt embarrassed by what she'd admitted. How couldn't she be? The kid had caught her acting as Kayleigh. He'd caught her in a lie she'd been telling herself for... well, she didn't know how long exactly.

But it was a lie that just made her feel a little more comfortable. A little safer.

A little less alone.

And a little less guilty.

"What about the dog?" Billy asked.

Aoife's stomach sank when he said those words. "I never saw Rex again."

"So he could still be alive."

Aoife shook her head. "He's gone."

"But you didn't see him—"

"He's gone, Billy."

She regretted snapping again right away. She knew Billy was only trying to reassure her, bless him.

But he was wrong. She couldn't live with any shred of hope. Not now.

He was gone. And Kayleigh was gone. And everything that gave her life purpose and meaning in the form of Sanctuary was gone too.

"This place," Billy said. "With... with the power. You said there were other places like that?"

Aoife felt her stomach tense up. She figured things might go in this direction. "There... there are some. But they aren't safe. I found that out for myself."

"But maybe the other places are different," Billy said.

Aoife shook her head and stood up. "We don't have time for this, Billy."

"But where better are we going to find?"

"I'm going to find somewhere safe enough for you," Aoife said. "And when I find it... I'm going to let you stay there. And then I'm going to go my own way. Because... because I don't want to stay in one place anymore. I don't want to settle down anymore. I don't want any of that responsibility. I'll look after you. I'll get you to where you need to go. But once we're there... once we're there, that's where you and me end. It's the way it has to be. I'm sorry."

She felt bad for saying those things right away. But she was being honest. She couldn't settle down anywhere where there were other people, another community, or anything like that. She didn't want to experience warmth and connection again. Because she'd experienced all that before. And she'd lost it.

And she knew just how painful it was to have something and lose it.

Billy lowered his head. He looked sad. But at the same time... there was an acceptance to his face. A look of acceptance that broke her.

"I'm sorry," Aoife said. "I don't... I don't say these things to upset you. I just... I don't... I can't look after you, Billy. For now, yes. But not forever. Not because I don't want to. But because... because everyone I've looked after is gone. Everyone I've been close to, I lost. Bad things happen to people I care about. Which is why I need to get you someplace safe as soon as possible."

"Then take me to one of the places with power," Billy said.

Aoife shook her head. "Nearest one is Wales, the last I heard. Or up in Scotland. It's way too far."

"Then where else is there?"

Aoife thought, but she was struggling. There were, of course, a few groups and communities she'd come across, some of which seemed better than others. But there was still a reluctance there. Still a sense that Billy would be safer with her than he would with them.

She needed to get her act together and make her mind up. Fast.

"I'll need a little time to figure that out," Aoife said. "But right now... right now we need to get moving. We can't afford to stand still. Not anymore. Especially not with what happened back at the pub. Ramiro's not so far away. And if he found us last time, he could find us again. We need to keep going."

She held out a hand to him. Saw the way he looked at it, then up at her.

And then he took it. Lightly.

"I wish..." he started.

"You wish what?"

"Nothing. It doesn't matter."

"You sure?"

He was quiet for a few seconds. And then, with a maturity that exceeded his years, he said: "I wish you didn't think losing everyone was your fault. And I wish you didn't feel so bad for... for imagining Kayleigh and Rex. To stop yourself being lonely. I do it all the time. Sometimes... sometimes I think I might still be back there, in Ramiro's. And that I'm just imagining all this like it's a big adventure. But that I'm... I'm gonna open my eyes, and it'll be dark again, or there'll be someone... there'll be someone..."

He stopped. She knew what sort of thing he was going to say. What sort of awful memory he was repressing. She didn't want him to have to go there if he didn't want to.

And she knew right now, as much as she was reluctant to commit to any long-term set-up, she had to look after Billy. She had to focus on getting him somewhere safe.

She could figure out where as they walked.

But for now, they needed to walk.

She tightened her grip on his cold hand. Squeezed it, just a little tightly.

"Come on," she said. "We'll figure this out. One way or another."

In the back of her mind, she swore she heard Kayleigh's voice, shouting at her from in the distance but fading further and further away...

CHAPTER TWENTY-FIVE

Ramiro looked out into the rain and tensed his fists so fucking tight he felt like his fingers might just break.

It was pissing it down, and he felt furious. Really fucking furious. He was at the shed in the garden behind the pub. He could see a little blood in there and footsteps in the grass, too. A trail.

They'd hid in here, Billy and that bitch. They'd climbed the fence behind the pub, and then they'd hid in here, and then when Ramiro and his people had walked on past, they'd run out of here.

They should never have been allowed to do that. They should never have been allowed to even get *close* to escaping the way they had.

They just kept slipping their way through Ramiro's fingers.

But that was going to change.

"I'm sorry, boss," a voice said. Kurt. That bastard who'd screwed up once today already, and now he was at it again. "We... we didn't even see the shed."

"How didn't you see the shed?" Ramiro asked.

Kurt lowered his head. He was totally drenched in rain. He was always a pale chap, but he looked like he'd gone another shade of white right now. Almost like he knew what was coming. The poor bastard.

"I swear," Kurt said. "Things were... things got complicated."

"Things didn't get complicated," Ramiro said, trying to keep as calm as he could. "What happened is, you let a woman and a kid run away. A kid who belongs to us. And a woman who has killed our own. And not for the first time today."

"I'm sorry."

Ramiro walked towards him. Four more of his people watched closely but looked away whenever Ramiro looked right at them. He liked that sense of power he had. That sense of fear he could instil in others. It was something he'd never had in his life before, a life of being pushed down, of being patronised, of being talked down to.

He liked how his life was now.

Leadership.

"I know you're sorry," Ramiro said. "I know you really, really mean that."

He put a hand on the back of Kurt's neck. Felt him flinch.

The fear was fucking electric.

"But there comes a point where apologies aren't enough."

He looked around at Dylan. Nodded at Kurt.

Kurt's eyes widened. "No. Please."

"On your knees," Ramiro said.

"Ramiro," Kurt begged as Dylan came over, dragged him down, got him onto his knees, then started stripping his clothes away. Stripping them and throwing them to one side, over into the snow.

Ramiro stood there looking down at Kurt. Getting harder and harder the more he looked at his cold, shaking body. It was that sense of fear in his eyes that really did it. That sense of knowing. Knowing what was coming next. Knowing exactly what Ramiro was doing to him.

Because he'd seen it done before.

He'd been a part of it before.

Ramiro pulled out his knife.

Kurt shook his head. Tears crawled down his face. "Please. I'm begging you. Think of—think of my children. Please."

Ramiro smiled when he said that, saliva trickling down his pitiful face. He walked over to Kurt, and he grabbed him by his hair. "Poor choice of words," Ramiro said.

"You're sick," Kurt said. "You're—you're a fucking sick monster. And you need stopping. Someone—someone stop this!"

But Ramiro's people just stood there. Pinning Kurt down. Not arguing. Not standing up at all.

Just complying with Ramiro's commands.

Ramiro looked into Kurt's eyes, and he smiled.

"It looks like nobody's listening today," Ramiro said.

Kurt shook his head. Tears streaming down his snivelling face. "Please."

"Unlucky," Ramiro said.

Then he nodded at his people, and they pushed Kurt down to the ground, face-first in the snow.

Ramiro lifted his knife.

Stared down at Kurt's bare ass.

"Keep still," Ramiro said. "You know this is far, far more painful if you resist."

"Please," Kurt groaned. "Please!"

And then Ramiro pulled back his knife and buried it deep into Kurt's ass.

CHAPTER TWENTY-SIX

I t didn't take Aoife long to find a community.

She squinted into the distance. Looked like it had housed an old American-style diner once upon a time. Walls had been erected through whatever scraps of metal were lying around. Coiled barbed wire marked the top of the fences. The entrance to the place was a rusty old metal shipping container with the doors open at either side. Aoife couldn't see inside the community from here, but she could see a couple of men standing on a building roof over to the right. A couple of people standing out front, next to a pair of dusty old leather sofas and a fire. She wasn't sure about this place. She wasn't sure about *any* place. But this one looked particularly decrepit and barren.

Didn't look the safest place, that was for sure.

But was it safe enough?

Fuck. That's a question Aoife had to answer for herself.

She looked around at Billy, who crouched by her side. They couldn't just stay here. Eventually someone would spot them.

But at the same time, maybe that's partly what Aoife wanted.

For them both to be spotted.

For her to be able to run away and leave Billy here, where he could be safe.

But that was exactly the problem. She didn't know if Billy would be safe here.

"So you're just gonna leave me?" he said.

Aoife's stomach sank. It was like the kid was reading her mind. "I didn't say I was going to leave you."

"You said you're staying on the road. That... that you don't want to settle down anywhere."

"I know what I said."

"Then are you going to leave me?"

Aoife looked into his terrified eyes. She felt so sorry for him. He'd been through hell, and she'd helped him out of it, making him all kinds of promises about how she would look after him.

And now she was going to just leave him here?

Leave him with a bunch of people she didn't know?

People who could well be just as savage as Ramiro's people— or worse?

It didn't sit right with her at all.

But what the fuck else could she do?

She thought about the other districts. About the nearest one, which would be in North Wales. Miles and miles away. A journey that would probably kill them, especially in the thick of winter.

A journey that would bring back all her guilt, grief, and pain.

But then, wouldn't that be better in the long run?

She needed to snap out of her selfishness. Sure, she might not want to go live with a community again. She might not feel deserving of it, or whatever.

But she owed it to this boy to find him the safest place possible.

She looked down at that community. The heavy doors to the container were open. Through it, she could just about see the rusty remains of a caravan and smoke.

"I don't like it here," Billy said.

"Well, sometimes... sometimes beggars can't be choosers."

"I want to stay with you."

Aoife looked around at him. Saw him staring back at her, right into her eyes. "That's... that's not possible."

"You promised me," Billy said. "You said... you said it might not be safe with you. And that it might not be comfortable. But— but you took me away from Ramiro, and you told me you were going to look after me."

"That was before..."

"Before what?"

"It doesn't matter."

"Before what?"

"It was before I started to... to properly care about you, okay? Before I started to worry about losing you. Because... because that's what'll happen if you stay with me, Billy. That's what'll happen. Something bad will happen to you, and I just don't know if I can live with that anymore. I don't know that I can live with losing someone else."

Silence followed. Aoife could barely even process the fact she'd spoken those words herself. She couldn't even look Billy in the eye. She was supposed to be the adult here, and she was confiding in this kid like he was her therapist.

She glanced at him. Saw him staring at her. Warmth in those innocent little eyes of his.

"Maybe I'm okay with that," he said. "Maybe... maybe I'd rather risk something happening with you than join some group where you're not with me. And that's... that's my choice."

She looked back at him now. Felt her heart racing faster.

And she felt such a connection and warmth with this kid that she could cry.

She opened her mouth, no idea what words were about to escape.

"I'm sorry," she said. "I…"

That's when suddenly, she heard footsteps, right behind her.

She saw Billy's eyes widen.

And then she heard a gruff, deep voice. "Don't move."

CHAPTER TWENTY-SEVEN

It wasn't long before Aoife found herself in familiar surroundings—locked away in darkness, hands tied behind her back, tied to the chair, and gagged.

She was really getting fucking sick of being locked away like this. How many times was this going to happen to her, and when would the day come when she wasn't going to get out of it?

She hoped today wasn't that day.

She looked across the caravan, over at Billy. It was a cleared-out trailer. The windows were curtained. The floor was sticky and grimy. It was damp in here and freezing cold. She looked around for some way out. It wasn't the most restrictive place she'd ever been tied, so she was sure she could get out of here if she really put her mind and energy towards it.

But then what?

They were right in the middle of a damned community. Not a big community by the looks of things, but a community all the same. There was a guard right by the door. She had no weapons. And even if she did use something, she'd only end up getting herself in deep shit for it.

She should never have come here. She'd put Billy in danger by coming here.

He was right. They should've just made a break for one of the districts. As much as the thought terrified her, at least she knew those places were … well. Safer than the vast majority of places.

Or she should have just looked after him. Let him travel with her…

No life for a kid.

But now he might not have any choice at all.

She pulled at the cuffs around her wrists, but it was no use. She'd fucked up. Big time. Only way she was getting out of here was by some miracle that the people who'd captured them both were the diplomatic kind.

And truth be told, they didn't seem all that friendly when they'd dragged her and Billy in here, accusing them of spying.

She looked over at Billy. Tried to say something to him, but her gag stopped her. She just wanted to reassure him. Reassure him everything was going to be okay. That everything was going to work out, one way or another.

She wasn't fully sure she believed it herself. That was the scary thing. She wanted to reassure this kid because she wanted him to feel better about this situation.

But she didn't feel good about their chances here. She didn't feel good about any of this.

She just hoped this group weren't the kind of psychopaths she feared they might be.

She looked across the room at Billy. Stared into his eyes. It was all she could do. Almost as if she could communicate with him this way.

I'm sorry. I'm sorry I couldn't be stronger for you. I'm sorry I couldn't be what you need. But I'm here. I've got you. This is going to work out. I promise this is going to work out.

She saw him turn his head, glance away like he wasn't hearing what she was thinking. Of course, he couldn't. She was crazy for even *trying* to transmit her thoughts to him or whatever the fuck she was doing.

She just felt bad about him ending up in this situation. Bad about how resigned he looked. Almost as if he knew it was an inevitability that he'd end up in some sort of captivity again. In some sort of shitty situation.

She didn't want it to be an inevitability. She wanted there to be an alternative for him. A real alternative.

He deserved that. Especially after everything he'd been through.

She looked around and took a deep breath through this stinky rag stuffed in her mouth. She wondered how many other people this towel had been stuffed in the face of. She dreaded to think. Cleanliness and hygiene weren't really a part of this world, and they certainly didn't seem a part of this community.

She closed her eyes and took in another breath. She found herself trying to find Kayleigh. Trying to search her down, speak to her, ask for her opinion, and see what she thought.

But there was nobody there.

There was nobody there except her anymore.

And it was a lonely place to be.

She opened her eyes and saw the door to the caravan swing open.

Bright outside. Super sunny day now.

Standing at the door, a woman.

Tall. Thin. Long, dark hair. A mean, serious look on her face.

"What do we have here?" she said.

oife stared up at the woman standing at the caravan door, knife in hand.

She was tall. Looked like she was in her late forties or her fifties; hard to tell. Long, dark hair interspersed with greys. Slim. Looked well for her age, in all truth.

But she had a serious look on her face.

And, yeah, that knife in her hand didn't exactly signal the friendliest of people.

She walked into the caravan, looking between Aoife and Billy. The door closed behind her. Aoife caught a glimpse outside—of the men standing around a fire in the middle of the barren interior of this place. But then the door closed, and she didn't get any more time to weigh up her surroundings—or figure out how easy or difficult it might be to get out of here.

She stood there a few seconds. Hands on hips. Staring at Aoife, now.

"Sorry for your introduction," she said. "But we can't be too careful. Rico says you two were watching us for quite some time. Like you were scoping us out. Fancy explaining that to me?"

Aoife stared up at her. Obviously couldn't open her mouth and speak because she was fucking gagged. Did the dumb bitch not realise that?

Right on cue, she walked over to Aoife. "My apologies. Let me help you with that."

She yanked the rag out of her mouth with force, making Aoife heave. Long, stringy saliva oozed out of her mouth as she coughed and spluttered.

"So now you're free to speak, why don't you start by explaining yourself?"

Aoife looked up at her. Her eyes burned up, streaming. "You could've fucking asked us this before dragging us in here and tying us up."

The woman stared at her. Coldly. Didn't seem to react to Aoife at all. "It's like I said. You can't be too careful these days."

"Well, I just think—"

"You can stop the cocky remarks and start by telling me who the hell you are and why the hell you're watching this place. Because believe me, I won't give you another opportunity to explain yourself."

Aoife tensed her jaw. She knew she had to be careful here. "I... I came here because I was looking for somewhere safe."

"You don't look like the kind of woman who has a permanent home, let's say."

"I'm not a kind of woman who needs a permanent home," Aoife said. And she tensed up even more. Because she wasn't sure what she was going to say next. Wasn't sure which path she wanted to take.

But in the end, she figured she had no choice but to be honest.

"The boy here, though. I... I was looking for someplace for him. People who can look after him. But now I see you've got your work cut out, and we'll be on our way."

The woman narrowed her eyes. Glared right into Aoife's.

"And I'm supposed to just believe you?"

"You can do what you want," Aoife said. "It's the truth. I got this kid away from... from a nasty situation. From some bad people. I'm trying to find somewhere for him. Somewhere safer. Somewhere better. But it's like I say. I can see this doesn't quite pass the test here."

The woman smirked at that. Nodded. Aoife wasn't quite sure why, but it seemed to tickle her. "And you didn't see the sign on the way in?"

"The sign?"

The woman shook her head. "Doesn't matter."

She was quiet for a few seconds. Still. Her focus was on Billy now. The way she stared at him made her feel... weird.

"Come on," the woman said. "There's something I want to show you."

She walked over to Aoife. Untied her from the chair, yanked her to her feet. Aoife tried to stand her ground, tried to dig her heels in.

"Hey," the woman said. "I told you to follow me. There's something I want you to see."

"Not without the kid."

"Trust me," the woman said, glancing at Billy then back at Aoife. "Where we're going, you don't want the kid to see."

Aoife looked around at Billy. Saw him shaking. Staring on with this traumatised expression of pure fear.

"It'll be okay, Billy," Aoife said. "I promise it'll be okay."

But she wasn't sure she believed herself.

The woman dragged her out of the caravan, out into the bright sunlight. It really was a barren place here. That fire burning in a rusty metal barrel right in front of her, two men standing around it, one of them with a rifle over his shoulder. A few chickens wandering around here and there. A small, quiet group of people. And yet a sense that something just wasn't quite right here.

"Where are we going?" Aoife said as the woman led her through the street, holding her arm.

"Just up ahead," she said.

"If you're going to kill me, can you just give me a heads up, so it's not too much of a shock?"

The woman laughed. "What would the fun in that be?"

She pulled her further through this empty wasteland of a community. Didn't seem like a home. More like an outpost, of sorts. The people standing on the diner roof up ahead, looking outside. And so many of them standing in front of shipping containers. Almost like they were guarding something.

Aoife wondered what was hiding inside them.

They took a right. Took Aoife a few seconds to realise they were heading through the shipping container that she'd come in through, back outside. And that's when her stomach sank even more. The realisation. The realisation that this woman was taking her outside to kill her. It had to be that. There could be no other explanation.

She felt the woman's hand press harder on her back. She was practically forcing her through this dark tunnel now.

"Go on," the woman said. "It'll soon make sense."

Aoife looked back at the inside of the community.

Back at that dirty trailer Billy was in, all on his own.

And then she took a deep breath, hoped for the fucking best, and turned back around.

The woman pushed her further outside.

Out of the community.

Towards the hill they'd come from.

And then she stopped.

Aoife looked around. Saw the woman standing there. Hands on hips. Half a smile on her stern, serious face.

"What is this?" Aoife asked.

"You really need to learn to read the signs, buddy," the woman said.

"What..."

And that's when it clicked.

The sign underneath the ad for the diner.

The sign that must've been blocked from view when she was up on the hill, scoping this place out.

The sign that sent shivers up her spine.

Water.

Coke.

Slaves.

CHAPTER TWENTY-NINE

Aoife looked at the sign, and her stomach sank.

Water.

Coke.

Slaves.

It clicked. Dawned on her immediately. The realisation of what this place was. The explanation for why it was so quiet and why it was so damned unusual, for want of a better word.

It was a trading point. Some kind of trading point.

Water.

Coke.

Slaves.

"So now you understand why we didn't want you snooping around this place."

Aoife seized up. She couldn't believe the mess she'd walked into. The first community she'd stumbled across, and it was some kind of trading point. Drugs and slaves.

She thought about Billy, trapped away in that caravan.

"Please," Aoife said. Desperation coming over her. "That kid. He doesn't deserve—"

"It's not for you to decide what he does and doesn't deserve.

You know 'deserve' doesn't come into the equation in this world. Not anymore. It's just business, friend. Purely business. And at the end of the day, if people are willing to pay a price, then that's just the way things go now."

"You don't understand," Aoife said. "I... I got him away from a group who—"

"Quiet," the woman said, putting a finger over her lips. "Honestly, you just made things harder on yourself the more fuss you kick up. Now, be grateful. If you were snooping around, your punishment would've been far, far worse. Think of this as an opportunity. We have some really distinctive clients. Not all of them, but some of them. If you're lucky... well. If you're lucky, you'll be okay. So too will the kid. Billy."

Bastard. "Don't you say his name."

The woman smiled. "I don't mean to be direct. But you really aren't in the position to be bargaining right now."

She stood there. Heart racing. Staring at this woman. Just behind her, she saw the opening to the trading point through the open doors of that shipping container. The caravan just beyond, where Billy was being held.

"Come on," the woman said. "Back inside. We've got a client on the way, actually. I think he'll be very interested in the kid. You, not so much. But your time'll come."

Aoife lunged forward. And the woman grabbed her. Wrapped a hand around her neck. Tight. She was strong. Stronger than she looked.

"Trust me," the woman said. "You want me to be your friend. You want me on your side. I'm the one negotiating the best deal for you, after all."

She felt her hand tighten around her neck just for a second.

And then she loosened it and let Aoife go.

Aoife dropped to the ground. Fell to her knees. Spluttered and gasped.

"Now, come on. Back to your feet. It's about time we got back inside. Our guests are due to arrive in no time. They're late, in fact. Which isn't like them."

Aoife shook her head. She didn't like begging. Never had.

But there were situations where putting pride aside and begging was the only thing you could do.

The *strongest* thing you could do.

"I know how business works," Aoife said, her voice wheezy. "I know full well how the world operates now. Everybody does. I'm not saying I agree with it. I'm not saying *anything*. I just... I want to ask you to cut us some slack, just for one day. For the sake of two people. Or even... or even just the boy. Let him go. Let him find someplace safe. If I... If I have to end up with the worst client in your catalogue for that to happen, I'm willing to do that. Please."

The woman tilted her head. Half-smiled. "You really care about the boy, don't you?"

Aoife looked away. "It's... it's complicated."

"But you're not his mum."

"What?"

"You're not his mum. I can tell that much. I'm guessing he fell into your company. Just like he'll fall into someone else's company. And he'll be safe there. Whoever he ends up with... I'll make sure I pick well. I'll pick someone who'll look after him, just for you. Because I appreciate how direct you've been with me. And I appreciate how much you're willing to sacrifice for his safety. That's all I can offer you."

"What will they offer you in return?" Aoife asked.

"What?"

"What will they offer you in return for him? Because I... I can offer you more. Way more."

The woman looked down at her, crouched down, clutching her neck. "Wow. You really are a wildcard, aren't you?"

"If it's weapons you want, I can find those for you. If it's water or food... I can find that too. Even if it's people... I can find that for you."

And then an idea came to mind. An idea she hadn't thought of before this point. An idea that was risky. That might—and probably wouldn't—pay off. An idea that felt morally wrong.

But all she had right now.

"I can find electricity for you."

"What?"

"I know a place. Several places, actually. Places where they have electricity. Where they have power."

The woman snorted. "Bullshit."

"I'm telling you the truth. I can show you. It's a long journey, but I can take you there. You can see for yourself. Allow me that much, at least. Allow me some time to prove that what I'm saying is true. And if—if it's not enough, then it's not enough. But at least let me prove it to you. Please."

She stared down at Aoife. Her eyes had narrowed. She looked confused. "How do you know about this place?"

"It's a long story."

"Tell me the short version."

"I... I lived in one of those places for a while. It fell. Outsiders took the place, and it—it caved in on itself. I've been out here ever since. But there were more places. Places just like it. If you... If I take you to one of those places, you let the boy live there too. That's all I ask."

"And what will *you* do?"

Aoife paused. She hadn't thought that far ahead. "We'll figure that out. But we can worry about that when we get there. If you let us get there."

The woman looked around. Sighed. Shook her head. But she looked interested, at least. Like she was curious about what Aoife had told her. Like her interest had been piqued just enough to intrigue her.

"You'd better not be fucking me around."

"I can't promise what state this community will be in. But assuming all went to plan... it'll be in a good way."

"No more trading," the woman said, staring into space. "No more of this... just somewhere to call home. That's what I want. That's what all of us want. More than anything."

"You get there, and you'll be able to put the past behind you. All of it."

The woman sighed. Nodded, again. "I never thought I'd find myself agreeing to this. Never in a million years. But you know what? Screw it."

She walked over to Aoife. Put a hand on her shoulder. "The name's Polly," she said. "And you'd really, really better not be fucking with me."

Aoife nodded back at her. "Aoife," she said. "I won't let you down."

She hoped she could keep her promise.

CHAPTER THIRTY

Ramiro looked out at the empty streets, and he sighed.

There was no sign of Billy. No sign of that woman travelling with him either. They'd lost them both. Well and truly lost them both. A fuck-up of the highest proportions.

He tasted blood on his lips. He could smell it in the air, too. Some of it wedged beneath his fingernails. A memory of the screaming. Of the struggling. He felt guilty about that. Kurt was a good man once upon a time.

He'd served Ramiro well in his final moments. He'd taken his punishment like a man—a squealing pig of a man, sure, but a man all the same.

He thought about the look in his eyes as he lay there on his shaking knees, turning back to Ramiro, shaking his head, begging, and for a moment, just for a split second, Ramiro saw himself in his position.

He saw his dad behind him.

Saw him exacting the same punishment on him when he was just a boy.

He shook his head.

Pushed that thought away.

He didn't need to go there anymore.

He looked at the empty road. At the abandoned cars. At the thick snow. It was cold, and it was getting late. He'd been walking for far too long. They were going to be getting worried about him back home. Especially since they had deals to do. Trades to make.

He had a lot of explaining to do. But since they were this far out, they might as well go the rest of the way and explain themselves to those they were supposed to be dealing with.

"No sign of prints," Jerry said. "No sign of blood. No sign of anything. We need to face it, boss. The kid's gone. Chalk this one down to experience and move on."

Ramiro shook his head. He didn't want to accept that. Who the hell wanted to accept any kind of loss—especially one as great as that?

But at the same time... he knew Jerry was right. They were looking for a needle in a damned haystack. Sometimes, leadership was knowing when to give up. Knowing when to quit the fight.

And that moment was right now.

"You're right," he said. "The kid's gone. Maybe fate'll bring him back to us one day. But right now... we've just got to crack on. Kurt paid for this loss. He paid for this grave, grave error. No point chasing shadows. Back to business."

"So, back home?" Jerry asked.

Ramiro turned ahead and looked down the road. Looked right into the distance, over to those metal fences, which he could just about make out.

At that sign, right by the gates.

~~Water.~~

Coke.

Slaves.

He took a deep breath, and he smiled.

"Nah," he said. "There's someplace I want to drop by first."

CHAPTER THIRTY-ONE

Aoife stood outside the caravan, Billy by her side, and tried to figure out whether she could deliver exactly what she'd promised to Polly and her people.

It was getting dark. Freezing cold. But Aoife felt hot. Her face was burning up. Sweat trickled down her chin.

Opposite her, she could see Polly discussing the situation with her people. She could see a couple of men shaking their heads, clearly disagreeing with what she was suggesting. They kept on looking back at her, too, staring over at her, shaking their heads even more.

Aoife knew it was a hard sell. After all, what was she even selling? The chance to walk away from a place like this, a lifestyle like this. Sure, that had to be appealing.

But what if she couldn't deliver?

What if she couldn't give Polly what she'd promised?

Fuck. She'd cross that bridge when she came to it. Worry about that at another time.

Right now, she had to worry about the immediate problem of hoping Polly's people saw her logic.

She looked down at Billy. Saw him standing there. Staring

blankly into the distance. He wasn't gagged anymore. Neither was Aoife. Even the ties around their wrists had been taken away. They were under watch, after all. Well under watch.

Even if they made a break for it, they wouldn't get very far.

And everyone here knew it.

"Hey," Aoife said.

Billy glanced up at her, then looked away. She could tell he was disappointed in her.

"We're... we're going to get out of this. I promise. They're going to take you someplace better than here, and everything is going to work out just fine."

"But you won't be coming with me. Will you?"

Aoife's stomach sank. She could hear the accusation in Billy's voice. "Billy, we've discussed this..."

"You want to leave me behind. But you could just—you could come with us. You could come to this safe place too. You don't have to be on your own."

Aoife wanted to agree with Billy. She didn't want to argue with him. And she didn't want to let him down.

But she knew there was no way she was going to one of those districts. Because it wasn't safe for her to be there. To be around people. She'd only destroy the place. Lead to its downfall.

Billy was safer if he wasn't with her.

"It's like I said," she said. "We'll cross that bridge when we get there. But for now... let's just focus on hoping these people agree to it, okay?"

Billy nodded. Shoulders slumped. Poor kid. All he wanted was her support and company. And she wanted that too.

She just couldn't offer it to him. Because it was too risky. Too dangerous.

For him.

She looked ahead at Polly, at her people. Saw them arguing. Saw the men shaking their heads. Heard Polly raising her voice, shouting unintelligible things. She saw Polly shaking her head. Saw her looking over at Aoife.

And then she saw her start to walk over towards her.

Her stomach tensed up. She feared the worst. Maybe Polly's people hadn't agreed to her proposal. Maybe they saw right through it. And she couldn't fucking blame them. It was barely a plan, after all.

But she stood there. Held on to Billy's hand, which was loose, no grip and no emotion in it at all.

"It'll be okay," Aoife said. "It'll work out."

Who are you trying to convince? The kid, or yourself?

She pushed that thought away.

Shouldn't think like that.

Polly walked right up to her. Stopped. Stood there, silent, hands on her hips.

"Well?" Aoife said.

"This place," Polly said. "How far?"

"I lead the way. That's the deal—"

"Don't make me torture you for the information. Trust me. We're throwing you a branch as it is. How far?"

Aoife knew it was all or nothing, and Polly wasn't playing around.

She shook her head and sighed. "North Wales. Forty, fifty miles. Long way. Hard in the snow. But it's doable. It's manageable."

Polly nodded. "And if you fuck up. If you even slightly fuck up..."

"I'm not pretending I'm a miracle worker. All I can do is take you there. I can only try my best."

Polly looked away. Shook her head. Cursed under her breath. "A lot of my people are *not* keen on this."

"And that's good for them. It's good not to trust too easily in this world. We both know that."

"Yeah," Polly said. "Yeah, you're right."

She shook her head again. Sighed.

"But a wise fella once told me something. Sometimes in life, you've got to dive in the deep end and take a chance."

Aoife nodded. She couldn't actually believe it. Polly was agreeing. They were going to go to North Wales. They were going to spare Billy.

And what happened to her... well, whatever happened to her, happened.

"Get some rest," Polly said. "The pair of you. We've a long way to go tomorrow. And you'll be leading—"

"Hope I'm not interrupting."

A voice.

A familiar voice, over to the right.

Aoife looked around, and her whole world felt like it was crumbling right beneath her feet.

Ramiro stood there.

His people by his side.

Smile on his face.

"Hello, Polly," he said. "Sorry I'm late. I believe we've got a trade to make."

CHAPTER THIRTY-TWO

The second Aoife saw Ramiro standing at the entrance to the trading point, she knew she was fucked.

He had this big smirk on his face. Looked around with confidence. He didn't seem to have seen her or Billy yet. And she wanted to keep it that way.

She had to hide.

Somehow, she had to hide.

"Ramiro," Polly said. "You're late."

"Had a long day," Ramiro said. "Lost some property of ours on the road. But no bother. Nature of the beast. How's..."

He stopped, then. Looked right over at Aoife. Right into her eyes.

She prayed he hadn't seen her. Prayed he hadn't seen Billy. Even though he was looking straight at her, she just prayed for a miracle right now.

But that miracle wasn't going to be granted.

"Polly," Ramiro said. "It... it seems like we have a little problem here."

"I don't see any problem other than how late you are."

"The property. The property we lost on the road." He nodded over at Aoife and Billy. "That property is right there."

Polly looked around. Aoife saw the look of realisation on her face. She was clearly putting two and two together, connecting the dots of the story Aoife had told her.

She looked back at Ramiro. "Well. That's odd. Because they're right here, in our walls."

Ramiro's eyes narrowed. His smile twitched, just for a moment. "Don't fuck with me, Polly. You know it's not a good idea."

"All I know is these two are here, in my possession. And if you want to trade for them, well you'd better make a good offer."

Silence.

Ramiro standing there.

His people standing there.

"Why don't you ask Billy there what he really wants?"

Aoife looked at Billy. Saw the way he looked at the ground. That hold Ramiro had over him, the manipulative bastard. She just hoped it wouldn't rear its head again.

"Hear me, Billy?" Ramiro said. "What do *you* want, hmm? You want to come home and forget about all this? Or do you want to keep on making this worse for yourself? 'Cause it will get worse. Just you look. You tried getting away. You tried running. You tried escaping. But we'll always catch up with you, buddy. We'll always catch up with you. Don't you see you're just making it worse for yourself?"

Aoife looked at Billy. "You don't have to listen to him, Billy. You don't have to listen to a word he says."

"Don't listen to her," Ramiro said. "Listen to me. Right now. Where do you want to be?"

Billy looked up. He looked at Aoife. Then at Polly. And then right at Ramiro.

And Aoife braced herself.

She braced herself for the inevitable. Because you couldn't save someone as lost and as trapped as he was.

"Where do you want to be?" Ramiro asked. Smile on his face.

Billy opened his mouth.

Then he closed it.

Cleared his throat.

"With Aoife," he said.

A weight lifted off Aoife's shoulders. Right at the point where her stomach sank even more.

Ramiro's smirk dropped.

His eyes widened.

"What was that?"

"With Aoife," Billy said. Louder this time. Louder and far more confident than before. "I want to be with Aoife. I don't—I don't care about safety. I don't care about—about being looked after. I don't care about any of it. I just... I just want to be with Aoife. Not with you. Not with any of you."

Ramiro was silent. Polly was silent. Everyone was silent.

It was Ramiro who broke that silence, as expected.

"Well," he said. Trying to smile, trying to give off the impression of confidence, even though he didn't have any left in the tank. "That is a shame. Because you don't get a choice in the matter."

He started walking towards Billy when Polly stepped in his way.

Rifles raised.

The rifles of Polly's people, pointing at Ramiro, pointing at his people.

"Back away," Polly said. "Right this fucking second."

Ramiro lifted his hands in the air. "We're unarmed. Your people saw to that at the gate. And we had the decency to comply."

"Then you should know better than this. Back the fuck up. Right now."

"I'm here to negotiate, Polly. We've always negotiated well in the past, haven't we?"

"This negotiation's closed."

Ramiro laughed. Shook his head. "I think you're forgetting just how much you owe us."

"We owe you fuck all."

"Oh, really? Defending you against Jarrod's lot? After everything we did to help you? You owe us years' worth of coke and slaves after that. Just a shame you don't have any more water to go around."

Polly lowered her head. Aoife could tell she was struggling with this. She looked torn. Completely in two minds.

"Hand the woman and the boy over, Polly," Ramiro said. "You do that, and we can consider ourselves even. No more debts to be paid. What'll it be?"

Polly lifted her head. Looked into Ramiro's eyes.

Then turned back to Aoife and Billy.

Polly's people held their guns, pointed them right at Ramiro's.

"I'm sorry," Polly muttered, staring at Aoife. The most human and vulnerable she'd sounded since Aoife had met her.

Ramiro smiled. "Don't apologise. The bitch understands it's just business—"

"I'm sorry, Ramiro," Polly said.

She turned around.

Faced him.

Ramiro's face dropped. "What?"

"The woman and the boy are not for sale. There is nothing to negotiate. I'd like—I'd like you and your people to leave."

Aoife heard gasps all around. Gasps from Ramiro's people, but also shouts of disbelief from Polly's, too. People who clearly weren't on board with this.

Ramiro glared right at Polly. "You're making a huge mistake."

"Maybe so," Polly said. "But we're not open for negotiation. Not right now. We've given you enough for free. And we are grateful for your assistance against Jarrod's lot. But truth be told... you need us just as much as we need you, in the grand scheme of things. It's time we actually started trading. We're not the ants, and you aren't the fucking grasshoppers. Not anymore."

Ramiro looked past Polly. Right at Aoife, right into her eyes. For a moment, he looked floored. Completely and utterly shell-shocked.

And then he smiled. Winked.

"Rules are rules."

He turned around and walked away.

"Come on, boys. You heard the lady. It's time we left."

Aoife watched him leave. Watched his people follow, rifles still pointed at them.

And as she watched them disappear through those metal doors, she couldn't help feeling terrified about what was going to happen next.

Because as much as she was relieved, and as much as she was happy to still be here and to have Polly defending her... she worried she might just have started something.

A war.

CHAPTER THIRTY-THREE

"I hope you understand the fucking risk I've just taken by saving your neck."

Polly stood opposite Aoife and Billy. She was shaking. Clearly the adrenaline of the whole situation had still got to her.

She'd stood strong. She'd ordered Ramiro to leave. She'd told him to get away, and she'd defended her and Billy.

But at what cost?

Aoife wasn't sure. Not yet.

But she feared it might be significant.

"Thank you," Aoife said.

"Thank you? That's all you have to say? Do you realise what I've just done?"

"What do you want me to say?"

Polly grabbed her by the scruff of the neck. "I don't want you to *say* anything. I want you to deliver on what you promised me. On what you promised my people."

"I told you I can take you there. I can't promise you much more than that. As long as... as long as you take Billy there with you... that's all I ask."

Polly shook her head. "Right now, I couldn't really give a fuck who I take with me. As long as you get us there. Because... because we're not safe here. Ramiro's people, they aren't the type to just walk away. They aren't the type to just give up without a fight. And besides. He's going to be pissed. Really fucking pissed. Especially after all the shit with Jarrod."

Aoife wanted to ask about Jarrod, what the deal with him was. But she figured now wasn't the time.

Polly looked caught in a whirlwind.

"We need to get everyone, and we need to get out of here. It's not safe. Ramiro... Ramiro will be back here. He'll be back with more people. We can't let that happen."

"You don't get to just make decisions like that," a voice said.

Polly looked around. Aoife saw a man behind her. Bearded. Tall. Sounded Eastern European.

He was holding a rifle. And there were a couple of people beside him too, who looked on his side.

"Jon..." Polly said.

"Don't give me that shit," he said. "You don't get to just do what you did without consulting us. All because of, what? The bullshit this woman's telling you?"

"Maybe it's not bullshit," Polly said.

"But maybe it is. We have a good thing going here. But you've screwed it. You've screwed it all. All for her. When she could be lying."

Aoife sensed the anger in the community. She could see the amount of people shaking their heads, shouting at Polly. She looked like a leader facing mutiny.

And she felt caught in the middle of it.

"Aoife here offered us a chance," Polly said. "A chance for a different way."

"And what if she's lying? Or what if she can't deliver what she's promising?"

"Then we'll cross that bridge when we come to it."

"Bullshit," Jon shouted. "This... this is bullshit."

He shook his head. And Aoife could sense anger in this community. People weren't happy with Polly. And as much as she'd bought her and Billy some time, she wasn't sure for how long.

And she knew she had to speak up. She knew she had to be honest. She couldn't just let this spiral out of control.

"I can't promise a miracle," Aoife said.

Everyone looked around at her. All fifteen, twenty people, staring right over at her. Like they were hanging on to her every word.

"All I can tell you is… is this boy here was put through hell by Ramiro and his people. He was put through hell by them for so long. I… I've been on my own for a while. Just wandering. I was in one of these places. One of these communities. Districts, they're called. And I know I can't convince you, and I know it sounds crazy, and I don't expect you to believe me. But I can take you there. I can take you to North Wales, and you can see it for yourselves.

"I don't even know what kind of state it'll be in. I don't know whether it'll still be standing. And you know what? Do whatever you have to do to me if that's the case. But… but all I'm asking is you give this boy a chance. Because he's suffered enough. He doesn't deserve to suffer anymore."

"And neither does she," Billy said.

His voice surprised her. She wasn't expecting to hear him speak up.

But he was standing right beside her, staring at this group of people.

"I… I was with Ramiro for… for a long time. I got away. And at first, I was scared. At first I… I kind of wanted him to find me. Because I couldn't make it on my own. But then… but then I found Aoife. I found Aoife, and she made me realise there's good people out there. And that I don't need a fancy home or anything like that. None of us do. Just as long as we have people who care about us."

He looked up at Aoife, then.

"So... so I believe Aoife. I believe her. And she'll take you to this place. And if we get there, and it's not what she thinks it is... then I'm with her anyway. Because I trust her. She's a good person. And I don't want her to be alone."

Aoife felt a lump in her throat. She looked at Billy, and she realised he wasn't just wanting to stick with her for her sake; he wanted to stick with her for *his* sake, too.

Aoife looked around at Polly. Then at Jon and the rest of her people.

"I'm sorry for the trouble we've caused you. But I promise if this works out... if this works out, then it'll be the best decision you've ever made. And if it doesn't... it'll be worth the risk anyway."

Polly shook her head. Sighed. "I can't believe I'm saying this, but we're with you."

She looked around at Jon. Then at the rest of her people.

"I am the leader of this place. And right now, we have an opportunity. An opportunity for a better life. A truly better life. And it might not work out. But at least we'll no longer be under Ramiro's thumb. At least we'll no longer live in fear. At least we have a real chance to start again. Because this. Slaves. Drugs. It's... it's not us. It doesn't define us. It doesn't have to be us."

Some people clapped. Some nodded in agreement.

And Aoife sensed the mood was shifting.

She sensed things were actually turning in her favour.

Polly looked around at Aoife, and for the first time, she smiled.

"We're going to try something different. We're going to try—"

A bang.

Blood spurting out of Polly's head.

Her eyes rolling back into her skull as she fell to the ground.

Shouting.

Crying.

Shock all over.

Jon stood opposite her, holding his rifle in his shaking hand, staring down at her twitching body, bleeding out on the dusty ground.

"No," Jon said. "That's not how things are going to go."

oife looked at Polly lying there on the ground, and she still couldn't quite believe what she'd just witnessed.

She lay there on her side, twitching. Her eyes had rolled back up into her head. Blood oozed out of her skull. She could still hear the gunfire echoing around. Hear people shouting, gasping in shock.

And she could see Jon standing there, staring down at her, wide-eyed like even he couldn't quite believe what he'd done.

He looked over at Aoife. Then around at his people.

"I had to do that," he shouted. "I—I didn't want to do it, but I had to do it, and you all know it."

Several people had their rifles raised. Pointed over at Jon. But a few of them were pointed at each other.

It was chaos.

"Polly's put our people in danger," Jon said. "She's put all of us in danger. She… she was a good leader. But what she was proposing was suicide, and you all know it."

Aoife held on to Billy's hand, which was shaking.

"It'll be okay," she whispered, without entirely believing it. "I promise it'll be okay."

"You killed her," someone shouted. "You—you don't get to just decide like that—"

"And let her take us all away from here? Let her take us on a journey someplace where we don't even know where we're going? Where we don't even know what's at the end of it? You really think that's the best option here? The most sensible option?"

"But—"

"I didn't want to have to do it. But she left me with no choice."

Aoife's heart raced. She wanted the world to open up, to swallow her whole. She couldn't stop staring at Polly's twitching body.

For all her flaws, she'd defended Aoife. She'd chosen to believe her.

And now she was dead. And her one ally here was gone.

She hoped more people here would see her side of things. That they'd come to her support. That they'd help her out.

But that didn't seem to be happening.

"So what do you propose we do?" someone shouted. "What the hell happens now?"

Jon's eyes widened even more. Like the sudden weight of increased responsibility was only just catching up with him.

"We ramp up our drugs trade," he said. "And we… we go harder on the slaves. You know that's where business really is. We all do."

"And what about them?"

It didn't take Aoife long to realise they were talking about her and Billy.

Jon looked at them. His nostrils twitched.

"They could be a bargaining chip," someone said. "We could use them to get something from Ramiro."

"No chance," someone else shouted. "Hand them back over. They aren't our problem. Ramiro won't rest until he gets what he wants."

Aoife could see Jon mulling his options over. She could see how torn he was. The devil on both shoulders. The possibility of greed taking over.

"One way or another," he said. "We need to get them back to Ramiro. We can decide the details on the way."

"We need to run," Aoife whispered.

"What?"

"We need to run. Now."

She knew it was the only shot they had. She knew they wouldn't shoot her or Billy because they needed them both.

She knew she had to make a break for it.

They both did.

She gripped Billy's hand tightly, and she ran over to the right.

"No!" Jon shouted.

She ran. Pelted over to the entrance door, the only way out of this place.

Come on. You can do this. You can make it. You can—

A blast.

The blast of gunfire, peppering against the ground all around her.

Keep going. Keep going. Keep—

And then she felt something slam against her back.

She flew forward.

Slammed face first into the dusty, cold ground.

She lay there a few seconds. Billy's hand still in hers. And for a moment, she wondered if she'd been shot in the back. She wondered if the pain just hadn't hit yet.

She looked around at Billy and realised someone was pinning them down.

She'd fucked it.

She'd had one opportunity to escape this place, and she'd fucked it.

She heard footsteps, walking right over to her, crunching against the ground.

She turned around, rolled onto her aching back, and saw Jon standing there, staring down at her.

"Bad idea," he said.

And then he pulled back his foot and booted her right in the face.

CHAPTER THIRTY-FIVE

Aoife felt herself floating.

She didn't know where she was. Didn't know how she'd got here. Wherever she was, it was dark. Pitch black.

But she was floating along. Floating in the darkness.

And there was a strange sense of peace. She wasn't quite with it, and she knew it. And she liked it that way. She wanted to stay in this place. This place where she had no worries. This place where she had no concerns.

This place where she had no responsibilities and didn't have to worry about a thing.

She looked around and realised it wasn't completely dark after all. She could see stars above. She was moving along the floor. Drifting along its surface. She was attached to something. Something dragging her along by the throat. And when she realised that was the case, she shook, tried to spin around, tried to gasp for air.

But she was trapped.

She was completely pinned down and trapped.

She saw figures. Figures alongside her. And then she saw a

chain from somewhere above her, attached to whatever it was she was being carried on, dragging her along.

And that's when she realised just how much shit she was in.

Polly's camp. The trading point.

Jon shooting Polly and telling his people they would make an exchange.

She knew what this was. Jon had kicked her in the head. She'd drifted in and out of consciousness ever since.

And now he was taking her back to Ramiro.

He was taking Billy back to Ramiro.

Shit.

Billy.

She looked around, her neck so achy, so sore. Tried to see Billy. Tried to find him.

But she couldn't see anyone at all.

Just the people dragging her along.

Just…

"She's awake," a voice said.

She felt herself stop.

Heard footsteps moving towards her, crunching through the snow.

And then she saw him, standing right above her.

It was Jon. Holding on to a rifle. Mean expression.

"Sorry about your face," he said. "But you really, really shouldn't have tried to run. Could've been a lot less painful if you'd just complied."

She tried to open her mouth to scream at the bastard, but she realised she was gagged.

"You have to understand it's not personal," he said. "It's just business. Really. You are Ramiro's property, after all. What Polly did, while noble, was wrong. So now it's our job to take you back. To deliver you to him. And the boy."

Aoife's stomach turned when he mentioned the boy. She

tensed up, tried to pull against the ties that bound her to this metal slab they were dragging her around on.

But it was no use.

She was stuck.

"At the end of the day... what Polly was proposing was mad for us. For the survival of our people. I don't doubt your intentions were good. But it's not our job to get caught up in the... morals, let's say. It's our job to trade. Water. Coke. Slaves. Whatever else we have. Polly's way has led to poverty for far too long. It's time for us to step up. And that starts with you."

Aoife wanted to scream.

"I am sorry you've ended up in the middle of this. Truly. I appreciate what you were trying to do. And I know you were thinking of your survival and the kid's survival. I understand that. But these are dangerous times, and you know that too. And there's far more dangerous groups out there than ours. Than Ramiro's, even. If Jarrod..."

He stopped. Trailed off. Jarrod. Not the first time she'd heard that name. Who was he? Clearly someone these people had trouble with. Someone Ramiro's group helped them fight, only to find them indebted.

Whoever the hell he was, he'd certainly caused a shitload of trouble, and his cloud still hung over this group's every decision.

"Anyway," Jon said. "We're almost here. I suppose I just wanted you to know I'm sorry. But that it's for the best. You're... you're sparing a lot of people by doing this. I know that's probably no great comfort. But it will be appreciated, and I will make sure of it."

I don't fucking care if it's appreciated. I want to rip your throat out, you traitorous bastard.

"Would you like to see the boy?" Jon asked.

Aoife wasn't sure what to do. What to say. Of course, she wanted to see him.

But at the same time... it was going to hurt if he looked like he was suffering.

"Bring him over, Trish."

She heard struggling. Shuffling. Rattling.

And then she saw Billy in the arms of a large, bulky woman.

He had duct tape over his mouth. His hands and feet were tied together.

Tears streamed down his cheeks.

There were bruises and scratches on his face.

"He's been quite a wriggly one," Jon said. "We've had to... step in, sometimes. I'm sure we won't have to do the same with you. Right?"

Aoife stared into Billy's scared, defeated eyes, and she wanted to apologise to him. She wanted to tell him how sorry she was for all this.

But then the woman dragged him back away, out of view.

She heard kicking out, struggling, punching.

She heard metal rattling.

And then she heard nothing, and she knew he was pinned down again.

"Right," Jon said. "We're almost at Ramiro's. I'll... I'll make sure this is as smooth as it can possibly be. For everyone. And sorry. Again. I... I mean that."

He looked at her, right into her eyes, and for one second, she swore she saw a flicker of guilt there.

And then he took a deep breath, turned away from her, and started dragging her across the ground again.

And there wasn't a thing she could do to fight.

CHAPTER THIRTY-SIX

Ramiro stared up at the stars, gritted his teeth, and braced himself for what he knew fucking well he had to do next.

He saw his people standing before him. Armed to the max. They'd lost some weapons to Polly's lot, sure. But that didn't matter. They had plenty more back home.

He still couldn't believe the arrogance Polly had shown by standing up to him. Bitch. She didn't know how lucky she was. Didn't know how lucky she and her entire group had been for so, so long. Especially after Ramiro bailed her out against Jarrod's lot three months back.

Well, she was about to find out how lucky she'd been.

"I know this is regretful," Ramiro said, looking at his people standing before him, illuminated by the burning barrels. "Polly's group have been close allies for a long, long time. But what Polly did today can only be described as an act of war."

Nodding. Muttering in agreement.

"There's no doubt the wider community is stronger for our allegiance with Polly. For the agreement we have with their people. And there's no doubt there will be... a domino effect, let's say. Consequences for standing against them. Other allies of Polly's. Those reliant on her trade. Things will change, that is for sure. And it will cost lives. There will be a human cost that we have to accept. That we have to live with if we're to go further. But we have to be willing to make these sacrifices if we're to grow stronger."

More nods. Claps. Shouting now.

Ramiro looked at his people, and he smiled.

"We march on Polly's camp tonight. We strike them. Hard. We give them no opportunity to stand with us. They'll be expecting us to give them a chance. They aren't going to get that chance. And that's where we hit them hardest. With surprise."

Shouting. Clapping. Some looks of uncertainty... but it wouldn't be long before they were all in agreement. All on board.

"We take their slaves as our own. We take their drugs as our own. But most importantly... whatever we do, we get Billy back. And we capture the woman who took him, too. I can't stress how important this is."

Ramiro saw them nodding and clapping, but he could see how uncertain they were, too. How unsure they looked.

They didn't understand just what Billy meant to him.

Just how wronged he'd felt.

Just how much he hated it when someone defied him.

That sense of power and dominance was way, way more important to him than anything else.

"We march tonight," he said. "We slaughter her, and we slaughter her people. Tonight is a new beginning, my friends. And it begins now!"

More cheers.

More applause.

More adulation.

And then Ramiro felt a tap on his shoulder.

"Sir?"

It was Keith. He looked shaky about something.

"What is it?"

"There's someone here," he said.

"Tell them to leave. We've got more important things to—"

"He says he's from Polly's group and that he has a delivery for you."

Ramiro turned around. "What?"

"He says he has a boy for you. Billy. And a woman. The one who took him. And he wants to trade."

CHAPTER THIRTY-SEVEN

Aoife wasn't sure how long she'd been dragged along the ground on a metal slab when she finally stopped.

She could hear talking. Chattering above. Some shouting, some commotion. And she got the sense that she was here. That they'd reached their destination.

Ramiro's place.

She tried to lower her head and squint to where she could hear the talking coming from, but it was no use. She was tied down. Didn't matter how hard she fought, there was no freeing herself from this bind.

She lay back, head against the metal slab. Not that she *wanted* to give up. But what the hell was she supposed to do now? There was nothing she could do. She wanted to fight free. She wanted to help Billy. She wanted to get the hell away from this place and start again, just the pair of them, away from all this mess.

But Jon had betrayed Polly, and now he'd brought her and Billy here to trade.

She just hoped things weren't painful for Billy. He'd stood up to Ramiro. Resisted. And she had to hope that didn't work against him.

Even though she feared he was going to be put through hell.

As for her...

Well. She'd given up. She'd accepted her fate. It was going to be nasty for her. Really fucking nasty.

But she'd handled shit before. Her nine lives were finally up. Whatever happened, happened.

Just as long as Billy was as comfortable as he could possibly be.

Out of nowhere, someone yanked her up. Snatched the ties away from her body.

"Come on," Jon said, his sickly-sweet breath strong in her nostrils. "We've got business to attend to."

Aoife looked ahead and saw Ramiro's camp. It was built onto a hill. There were several metal gates leading up a slope. Lots of people standing around on platforms that'd been built onto trees. In fact... shit. This was one of those old Go Ape places. The old zip-wire adventure parks. It looked like they were using the old activity platforms as watch towers. Clever.

A hand pressed against her back. "Go on. Move."

She snapped back into the present moment. Looked around at Jon, who stood there, shaking. He looked nervous as hell. That gave her a kick, at least. She wanted this bastard to be nervous. Any discomfort was a positive as far as she was concerned.

She wanted to ask him where Billy was, but she was still gagged. She turned and looked around. Saw Jon's people walking into Ramiro's lair through the gates, which were basically just steel panels that'd been propped up between the trees. There were several layers of gates, like the layers of an onion. It felt like this place was heavily protected. Perfectly designed to stop outsiders getting in.

Or to stop people on the inside getting out.

She felt Jon push her hard. She wanted to stand her ground. Wanted to dig her heels right in. Because this felt mad. She knew what kind of a man Ramiro was. If Jon started trying to negotiate with him... she feared things might not go as planned.

But she could only walk.

She walked through the first set of gates, which slammed shut behind her. Then through the next set. And the deeper she got, the more of a sense of scale she got about Ramiro's people and the operation they had going. There were lots of them. Armed. Mostly men.

All checking her out with toe-curling interest.

She felt Jon push her harder. Walked along, wondering where Billy was. She could see more of Jon's people up ahead but couldn't quite make out Billy. He must be up there. He had to be.

"When I say I'm sorry for what's going to happen to you," Jon muttered. "Believe me. It's not personal. But it's business. And it'll be better for all of us if we have a peaceful exchange here."

Bastard. I'll show you a peaceful fucking exchange if you let me go…

She kept on walking, further into the belly of the beast. The snow here was slushy and muddy. The place felt filthy. It just felt dirty to even be here. The smell of weed in the air. The taste of sweat.

And then she went through another gate, and she saw something that made her heart skip a beat.

A kid. Little girl. No older than sixteen, surely. She was wearing barely anything at all. Shivering away.

She had a chain around her neck, and a massive man beside her was dragging her along.

Like she was a dog.

Aoife's fists clenched. Her blood boiled. The fuckers. These fuckers were savages, and they deserved hell for this.

She thought of Billy and pictured him with a chain around his neck, shivering away, skin icy blue with the cold.

Thought of the dead, resigned look in his eyes, just like the girl.

A look that came when fear had gone away, and all there was left was simply existing.

"I don't condone what they do with them," Jon muttered.

"None of us do. But it's their business. It's just the way the world works."

Cunt. Give me five minutes with you, and I'll show you how the fucking world works you snake.

She saw a small group up ahead. Jon's people.

And beside them, right in front, Billy.

She felt relieved to see him. But she felt sad, too. Sad that she'd not been able to protect him. Sad that she'd got him in this mess in the first place.

It'll be okay, she thought, trying to convince herself more than anyone. *I'll find a way. I have to find a way…*

But she knew she was only fooling herself.

Suddenly, she stopped. Standing in the middle of this more open section of woods. Wooden picnic benches around. An old, sheltered area. A little cabin to her right, probably the reception hut of this Go Ape place, back in the day.

Ramiro's people stood around, watching. Staring closely. Very closely.

Aoife held still, looking around for any way out. For any weakness in this place.

But she couldn't see a thing.

She looked down at Billy, who stared at the ground.

It'll be okay, Billy. I made you a promise, and I intend to keep it. It'll be…

And then she heard a voice up ahead.

A familiar voice.

She looked ahead of Jon and his people and saw Ramiro stepping out, smile on his face.

"Well, hello," he said. "It looks like we have a bit of business to do, huh?"

CHAPTER THIRTY-EIGHT

"Well, isn't this a pleasant surprise," Ramiro said, smile on his face. "We really were starting to get awfully worried about you, Billy. Thought we were going to have to take matters into our own hands. But it looks like you've seen sense."

Aoife felt sick. All these eyes on her. Standing here in the middle of Ramiro's camp and knowing what sort of fate lay ahead. There was no way out. There was no escape for her, and there was no escape for Billy. She'd looked everywhere, but there was no chance.

They were stuck in here. Trapped.

And at this point, Aoife just had to hope and pray Ramiro didn't take out his anger on Billy too much.

Because this was on her.

It was her who had helped him escape.

It was her who'd helped him flee.

She didn't care what happened to her, just as long as Billy didn't suffer.

"Polly," Ramiro said. "Where is she?"

"She's dead," Jon said.

Ramiro narrowed his eyes. "Wow. Now that I was not expecting. Shame. Nice woman. Until our recent disagreement, anyway. Which I'm assuming this is about?"

Jon nodded. He looked afraid. Nowhere near the assertive confidence Ramiro had. "She—she put our people in danger. Jeopardised the agreement we had."

"You did the right thing, Jon," Ramiro said, smirking. Like this was all a big game to him and like he didn't take Jon all that seriously. "When a leader gets too big for their boots, they're in trouble. Polly made a mistake. A real big mistake. And she paid for it. But you're here. You're here, and you've prevented conflict between our people and yours. That's leadership. Real leadership. Now. Hand Billy and the bitch over, and we can be done. Move on from this sorry mess."

Jon stood still. He was holding onto Aoife's and Billy's arms. He was shaking.

"That's... that's not going to happen," Jon said.

Ramiro frowned. A few people gasped. What the fuck was he doing?

"What did you say?" Ramiro asked.

Jon cleared his throat. Clearly trying to sound a bit more confident, a bit more assertive. "Our people have been good to your people for—for a long time now. We've helped you. Given you what you've asked for. But... but we think we've repaid enough. It's time to start being fair again. Fair dealing. Still—still co-operating. But it can't be half of our drugs and supplies anymore. It's got to be fair trade. And unless you give us that... the kid and the woman stay with us."

Silence. Everyone staring at Jon and Ramiro. Even Aoife couldn't believe this was happening. Jon was getting too big for his boots. He'd tasted a bit of power, and now he thought he could start calling shots of his own.

Even Aoife knew that wasn't a good idea. Not with someone like Ramiro.

He wasn't going to like it. He wasn't going to like it one bit.

Ramiro smirked. Shook his head. "After all our help. After protecting your people against Jarrod. This is how you repay me?"

"We're grateful for your help against Jarrod," Jon said. "Truly. And that's why the fifty-fifty cut of all our shit went on so long. But it's gone on long enough. We're expanding, and we've hit a trade limit. So we want to re-negotiate. Twenty-five per cent. A quarter of what we have is yours. For... for, let's say, a year. Then we revisit it. That's fair. Surely you've got to see that's fair, right?"

Ramiro didn't say anything in return. He just stood there. Hands on his hips. Smiling. Looked in genuine disbelief.

"I've got to give it to you," he said, walking over to him. "You've got balls to come into my home, to give up your arms, to stand there with *my* property and start using them as a bargaining chip. I'll give you that."

Jon stared into Ramiro's eyes. He was clearly trying very hard to keep his composure but just as clearly shitting himself.

"You know what?" Ramiro said. "Seeing as you're in a negotiating mood, how about we try something else. How about you give us seventy-five per cent of your shit *and* hand over Billy and his bitch here?"

Jon shook his head. "What the fuck?"

"Or how about we go the whole way? You give us *everything*. How does that sound?"

"Ramiro," Jon said. "I'm not fucking around."

"You come into my home. You bring your people along. You get a bit too cocky and confident 'cause you're the leader all of a sudden. And you start trying to use *my* property to bargain? Come on, Jonno. Think about this. Is this really the road you want to go down? And thing very, *very* carefully before answering that question."

Aoife stared at Jon, heart racing. She could see the fear in his eyes. But also the determination. He'd had a taste of power. He didn't want to look weak in the eyes of his people.

"You—you get thirty per cent," Jon said. "Take it or leave it. But—but if you leave it, we walk away. I've got people outside. People who… people who'll act right away if you try anything. So don't—don't even think about it."

Ramiro stared at Jon.

Silence.

And then he laughed.

Shook his head.

"You know, I really, really hand it to you," he said. "You've got serious balls."

He looked around at Aoife, and then out of nowhere, his smile dropped away.

He pulled back a knife and rammed it right into Jon's chest.

Dragged Jon close, peered right into his face, right up close.

"But you're stupid. You're fucking stupid. You're a snake. And I could never deal with a pathetic excuse of a leader who kills his actual leader."

Jon shook. Gargled blood. Twitched as Ramiro propped him up.

"Me and Polly might've disagreed. But at least she had fucking principles, you piece of shit."

He let go of him.

Let Jon stagger forward and backwards, clutching onto his bleeding chest. Blood spurting from his lips as he fell to his knees.

Ramiro stood over him. Stared down at him with disgust.

"You did this," he said. "You. And nobody else. And the rest of your people will pay for it."

He looked around at a few of his people, and he nodded.

And suddenly, before Jon's people could run, gunshots.

Ramiro's people shooting at Jon's.

Slaughtering them.

Shooting them in the heads, shooting some of them in the legs, massacring them, capturing a small subset of them.

Screaming.

Shouting.

Panic.

Jon sat on his knees, Ramiro before him. Looking around at his people, all dying, all around him.

Ramiro smiling.

"Look around, Jon. You did this. This is where greed gets you. I would say take it as a life lesson. But... well. Ah well."

He pulled his knife back and buried it into Jon's throat.

Tore his neck from one side to the other.

Blood splattered out everywhere.

And then Ramiro kicked Jon back and onto the ground before him.

Gasping.

Twitching.

Staring up in fear.

Aoife looked down at Jon. She looked at his people lying dead all around him.

And then she looked over at Billy and then up at Ramiro.

He smiled at her. Blood dripping from the knife in his hand.

"Now," he said. "Where were we?"

oife stood in the middle of Ramiro's camp, gag around her mouth.

Jon lay dead before her. His body twitched. Blood trickled from his throat, bubbling on the ground, making the slushy snow even darker.

Beside him, Aoife saw more of his and Polly's people. Dead. Bullet wounds in their heads, their backs. Some of them weren't dead. She could still see them struggling for breath, lying there in agony.

But they were no threat to Ramiro. Not anymore.

There were others, too. Ones who had been captured by Ramiro's people. And it was those who she felt the most sympathy for, weirdly.

Because she'd seen just how ruthless Ramiro could be.

And she knew how much danger that put her and Billy in, too.

She looked around for Billy. Saw him standing there, head lowered, looking afraid. Usually had this resigned look to his face. Like something had died inside him 'cause of all the shit he'd been through.

But right now, he actually looked worried.

Because he knew he'd got himself in the shit by running away.

And he knew that would mean punishment.

"Sorry for the dramatics," Ramiro said, wiping his bloodied knife against his coat. "Although, if I'm honest, it should be you apologising for that, shouldn't it?"

Aoife clenched her fists. Her nails buried into her palms. She didn't break Ramiro's gaze. Not once.

He walked over to her. Smiling. "Quite a chase you've had us on. Thought we'd lost you. Then lo and behold, we come down to Polly's to do a deal, and who do we find? You. Waiting right there for us. Fate, isn't it?"

He got closer, and Aoife wanted to scratch his eyeballs out. She wanted to tear his throat away with her fucking teeth.

"But you know what? In the end, you've done us a favour. Polly's gone. And without Polly, that group was useless. She was the only wise head holding them together. Jon should've known that, bless him. But now there's a void there. There's a lot of drugs there. There's slaves there. And there's a real chance for us to expand. So thank you for helping us with that. For that, I'll be a little bit more forgiving about what you've done to us. What you've taken from us. Just a little."

She stood there, heart racing fast, throat tensing up. She felt a bit fearful, but mostly she just felt fucking mad. She felt mad at Ramiro for what he'd done and for what he was about to do. And she felt mad at Jon, too, for leading her into this mess.

She'd come so close to some kind of resolution when Polly was alive. Some kind of way out. A journey to one of the other districts—a journey she didn't *want* to do, sure—but a journey she knew she had to do. For Billy's sake.

And now, she was facing torture and almost certain death.

"Look at you both, all gagged like that. Let me help you with that."

He reached forward and tore the tape away from Aoife's mouth, a little too hard. Then he pulled the sock from her teeth and threw it to the ground, making her heave and splutter right away.

"That's it," he said. "Get it all out. I'll be helping Billy with his."

"Do not fucking touch him," Aoife gasped.

She tried to lunge forward, but someone held her back. And that seemed to make Ramiro smile even more.

"He's my property. I'll do what I goddamned want with him."

He walked away from Aoife, then. Went over to Billy. Untied the tape around his mouth and pulled his gag away.

He crouched opposite him. Smiled.

Billy stared at the ground before him. Didn't once meet Ramiro's gaze.

"You've been a real headache for us, y'know? A lot of people have died 'cause of your actions. A real shitload of stuff has gone down. You've been bad. Real bad. And you've gotta learn the consequences of your actions eventually."

Aoife surged forward again. "Leave him alone!"

Ramiro looked over at her. Put a hand on Billy's shoulder. But kept his focus on Aoife at all times. Smiling. "You know what happens to people who run," he said. "You know what happens to people who are naughty, right, Billy?"

Billy started shaking. Aoife could hear his teeth chattering.

"But it's like I say. As much as things have gone to shit... you've actually done us a favour, in a way. So you know what, Billy-bob? Maybe we can treat you instead. Treat you to a real welcome home. Because you've done good for us, boy-o. Real, real good."

A smirk crept up his face even more. Something sinister about it. Something that made Aoife feel even more protective, even more defensive.

"Please," she said. Not wanting to beg. Not wanting to appear weak. But wanting to protect Billy more than anything else.

Ramiro chuckled. "Shoulda thought about that before you kidnapped this boy, hmm? Made him say some hurtful things to me and my people. Some *real* hurtful things. But hey. We can forgive him. He's home now. And boy is he going to know it."

He glanced at one of his people beside him. "Deal with her."

He dragged Billy away, off towards the reception room over to the right.

Aoife tried to lunge forward again. "Don't fucking touch him! Don't you fucking touch him!"

But Ramiro just kept on walking away.

Billy's hand in his.

"Please! Please!"

Billy looked around.

Just once, he looked around and looked right into Aoife's eyes.

And for a moment, just for a moment, Aoife saw fear.

And then someone wrapped a hand around her mouth and dragged her back to the cold, bloody ground.

CHAPTER FORTY

Aoife sat in the darkness again.

It was similar to the other times she'd sat in the darkness. That fear. Wondering when someone would next come in here. Wondering whether she'd ever have the blindfold removed from her eyes. Listening to every single creak outside and wondering if they were coming for her.

And wondering when her time was up.

Because the difference about this time? What felt different now to the other times she'd been locked away and held in darkness?

This felt final.

This time, it felt like the last time.

This time, it felt like she was really dealing with someone who wasn't going to let her go.

And this time, she felt afraid, not for herself, but for someone else.

For Billy.

She thought of the fear she'd seen in his eyes during that last glance they exchanged. And she had no idea how long ago that was. It felt like forever, but it could be hours. Or days. Or weeks. Time had lost all meaning.

Only one thing was for sure.

Billy was going through hell at the hands of these monsters.

And that was on her.

She tried to imagine Max, Kayleigh, or Rex. But none of them would appear with any real clarity. She tried to escape to someplace else, somewhere safer in her mind, where Billy was there, and where everything was okay again.

But that place was gone. She couldn't get there. It's like accepting Kayleigh and Rex weren't alive and real anymore had closed a door in her mind, and she couldn't retreat there. Not anymore.

She wanted to cry. She wanted to scream.

But all she could do was sit here, on this chair, in the darkness, waiting for whatever was next.

She pictured Billy, and she saw Ramiro holding his arm. She saw the horrible brutes in here, the way they had that leash around the little girl's neck, treating her like some kind of animal, some kind of pet. She heard their laughter in her mind, and she tried to push it away. She tried not to hear it. Tried not to feel any of it.

But it was too late. The moment she imagined these things, they were here, and they were present, and there was no getting away from them, no escaping them, no hiding from them.

And she knew she was stuck with these taunting memories.

And then they got worse. The memories of the power source. The memories of Yuri, Kayleigh, and Sanctuary.

The memories of Max, burning.

The memories of Jason.

The memories of all she had and all she lost.

And she didn't want to pity herself. She hated self-pity. She wanted to step up, and she wanted to fight.

But she felt like everything she touched turned to darkness, eventually.

And now it was finally going to end, just as it was always destined to end.

Her, fucking things up for someone else.

Fucking things up for someone else before finally, finally getting exactly what she deserved.

She heard the door ahead of her clang open.

Heard a man coughing, then heard footsteps.

She sat there. Totally still. Waiting for whatever was about to happen to her next. It felt like she was sitting there forever.

And then she felt the man yank the blindfold from her eyes.

It took her eyes a moment to adjust to the light.

But when she looked up, blinked a few times, she saw him.

Ramiro was standing over her.

Smile on his face.

"It's about time we dealt with you," he said. "Once and for all."

CHAPTER FORTY-ONE

Billy sat in the dark and cried.

He kept his eyes closed 'cause he didn't want to see anything. When he opened his eyes, he saw the darkness, which scared him. He saw things moving in the dark. Monsters. The monsters under the bed he used to see. The ones Dad told him were okay, that they couldn't hurt him.

And he knew he was too old to worry about them now. He knew they weren't real.

But they *felt* real.

Everything *felt* bad right now.

He just wanted to be back outside with Aoife.

He just wanted everything to be okay again.

He tasted salty tears on his sore, chapped lips. He was stupid. Stupid for being such a big crybaby. He used to be tough. Strong. When he'd come to this place, he'd been scared at first. But then he'd got to the point where he went through so many nasty things that he wasn't scared anymore. He was numb. He was dead inside.

And then he got away, and he met Aoife, and it felt like he'd remembered what it was like to feel again.

To be a child again.

A person again.

But that was bad, too, because he felt weak, and he felt sad, and he felt terrified, and he just wanted to get away from this place.

He opened his eyes just a little. Total darkness. But he knew where he was. He'd stayed in here a lot. The dark room, all on his own. He knew there was no way out. He knew he was trapped here. And as much as he was scared of Ramiro and his people and how they would punish him for running away, he wanted someone in here. He felt alone, and he wanted someone to just tell him everything was going to be okay.

Or even if they didn't tell him that... he just wanted someone close.

Even if they were saying and doing the worst things in the world to him, he'd do anything to be near someone right now.

He heard movement in front of him. Rustling around. And it made him almost wee. Because it sounded like someone was in here with him. Watching him. Laughing at him.

He squeezed his eyes shut again. Heart beating so fast he could hear it in his ears. *Thump, thump. Thump, thump.*

And the more he focused on it, the faster it got.

He held himself tight.

You'll be okay. You'll be okay. You'll be...

And then he felt something.

Right against his leg.

Something touched him.

And he wasn't sure why, but it made him jump, and it made him scream and flip and punch and kick everywhere.

And then he heard squeaking.

A rat.

It was a rat.

Just a rat.

He calmed down with deep breaths, even though he was shaking, even though he was so, so scared.

"Sorry, Mr Rat," he said. "I was just... I was just scared. But it's okay. You can—you can sit with me. If you want."

He opened his eyes just a little bit. He couldn't hear scuttling or squeaking anymore. And he couldn't see any faint trace of the rat anywhere at all.

"Please," he said, his throat welling up. "I... I'm sorry. I just want somebody to talk to. I'm sorry. I was just scared. Please."

But the rat didn't make a sound.

Wherever it was now, it wasn't nearby.

Billy felt his sadness turn to anger.

He buried his head in his knees, and he screamed.

Screamed and tensed up.

Let a lungful of air out.

He just wanted this to end.

He just wanted this to be over.

He just didn't want to hurt or be sad anymore.

He stopped screaming when he was all out of breath. His chest felt tight. His heart was racing, and he was dripping with sweat, even though he was freezing cold.

"I just want to be a normal kid," he said. "I just... I just want Aoife now. I just want my friend now. Please."

He crouched there, squeezing his eyes so tight, hoping that if he did that, he'd just appear somewhere else, appear somewhere before all this. Or wake up from a nightmare. Or disappear into another world where everything was good, where everything was okay, where there was no sadness, not anymore.

He kept on squeezing his eyes shut and tensing up his body until he heard something.

A bang.

A clatter at the door.

The sound of something sliding open.

And then, footsteps.

CHAPTER FORTY-TWO

Christopher stood on the building at Polly's old place and stared out into the darkness.

It was a dark one. Cloudy. Particularly cold, too. Goddamned freezing. His fingers felt like they might just drop off. Teeth chattering away like mad.

But you know what?

He didn't really give a fuck.

'Cause today was a momentous day.

He looked over his shoulder, down at the inside of Polly's old community. Looked at the garage in the middle, the place where all the drugs were stashed. Then over at the caravans, where they kept the slaves. He smiled. It'd only been a few hours, but this was their place now. That stupid ass bastard Jon came walking into their home trying to bargain and make deals.

And where the hell had it got him?

Dead.

Dead, like so many of his people.

He turned around and looked back out into the darkness, rifle in hand. He knew Ramiro had eyes on this place for a while. But he always called Polly a "useful ally." 'Cause it was only together that they had enough about them to stay strong against other threats out there.

Threats like Jarrod.

He shuddered when he thought of Jarrod. He knew everyone here did. As much as he liked to pretend he was one big tough guy, even Ramiro was afraid of Jarrod.

'Cause they weren't as tough a group as Ramiro liked to pretend they were.

Sure, they were tough. Tougher than Polly's, but only by a little—and ironically only because of some of the trade and supplies Polly provided them with.

But without Polly's group... they weren't as strong as they once were. They were weaker now.

Far, far weaker against Jarrod than they used to be.

Which was why Christopher had been sent here. To maintain the illusion that Polly's people were still running this place.

'Cause if Jarrod found out they weren't, if Jarrod found out Polly was gone...

He shuddered. Didn't want to think about that.

He kicked a stone off the roof of the building he stood guard on and watched it fly over the edge into the darkness. Deep down, he knew he was supposed to just tow the line. But he was pissed at how Ramiro had acted. This mad chase for Billy, obsessive. It'd got them in a lotta trouble.

And then slaughtering Polly's people...

He'd weakened his own hand, and he knew it.

Christopher just hoped he knew what he was doing.

"Fucking shit here, isn't it?"

Christopher looked around. Saw Fraser climbing the ladder, approaching him. Fraser was an arsehole if ever Christopher had met one. Absolute sadistic dickhead.

Which Christopher knew was ironic. He wasn't exactly standing up against the shit Ramiro was doing, of course. The slaves. The kids... yeah, it was morally iffy, that was for sure.

But Fraser was a violent thug with an extra edge of cruelty to him. And Christopher didn't like him one bit.

He walked up to Christopher's side. Lit a cigarette. "Want one?"

Christopher shook his head. "Don't smoke."

Fraser nodded, smiled. "That's right. Never have smoked. Always forget that."

That's because you're a self-absorbed dickhead.

He puffed at that cigarette, looked back at the community. "You looked stressed, fella. Maybe you should try smoking."

"I'm not interested."

"Try something else then. You know. Plenty of women here. Compliant as fuck, too. Like they've had the resistance fucked out of 'em, know what I mean?"

Christopher felt sick. As much as he was a part of Ramiro's group, and as much as he'd seen and been responsible for some horrible shit, that was a line he did not cross.

"Oh, come on, pal," Fraser said, slapping him on the back. "Lighten up. You stand around like you've got it bad. Let your hair down a little and chill."

Christopher felt his jaw clenching. Bastard. If he didn't shut up, he'd throw him off this fucking roof.

"We're supposed to be doing a job," Christopher said.

"And what the fuck you think's gonna happen if you take a few minutes off for yourself? Besides. They're that desperate for it to end, they'll be cumming in seconds. Just you watch, I've seen it—"

Christopher grabbed Fraser by the scruff of his neck.

"Whoa," Fraser said, raising his hands. Smile on his face. "Whoa. Chill yourself out, buddy. Chill yourself the fuck out. I could knock your fucking teeth out and crush your fucking skull. Get your hands off me, right this fucking second."

Christopher held on to him. But then he found his grip loosening. Found himself letting go. 'Cause Fraser was right. As much as he'd love to throw this bastard off this roof, he was stronger than him. He needed to pick his fights better than this in future.

He let go of Fraser. Stepped away. Went to turn around, to look back over the side of the building and into the darkness, when out of nowhere, he felt a splitting pain crack against the side of his head.

He fell down and hit the roof.

Turned around and saw Fraser standing over him.

"Bastard," he said.

"Fraser—"

Fraser booted him in the stomach. Hard.

Then he reached down and grabbed his throat. Tightened those big, heavy hands around him.

Squeezed.

Harder and harder.

Staring down at him with manic, bloodshot eyes.

"I'll teach you some fucking manners," he said, dragging him over to the side of the building and holding him over it.

Christopher slapped at Fraser's hands, tried to break free, but it was no use.

He couldn't breathe.

He was trapped.

"I'll teach you a fucking thing or two," he said. "You nervous, scummy little worm."

He gripped Christopher's throat so tightly he thought it might burst.

"Frase... Fra..."

He saw colours in his eyes.

Ears ringing.

Fraser holding on.

And then he heard something.

A bang.

A sudden bang out of nowhere.

And for a moment, he thought it might be his own throat, splitting under the force of Fraser's grip.

But then he saw something above him.

Drifting. Hard to make out.

But through the colours, through this haze...

He saw blood pooling from Fraser's head.

The top of his skull had been blasted apart.

His brain dangled out like a snail emerging from its shell.

He fell flat onto Christopher, pinning him down with all his weight.

And Christopher didn't get it. He didn't understand.

He looked around, and then he saw something.

Or rather, some*one*.

Someone standing at the gates to this place.

And when he saw who it was, the momentary relief he'd felt at Fraser's death was quickly replaced by fear.

Total fear.

This was bad.

This was really fucking bad.

CHAPTER FORTY-THREE

Aoife wasn't sure how many times Ramiro's fist cracked across her face before she finally stopped caring.

The pain was excruciating; make no fucking mistake about that. All she could taste was blood. Whenever she tried to breathe, tried to catch her breath, Ramiro just punched her, again and again and again.

But she'd reached a point where she knew that as long as he was in here, he wasn't hurting Billy.

And it was the small victories that mattered now.

She tried to break free, but it was no use. She was tied to the chair. No way out at all. She'd tried to resist, tried to fight, tried to figure out a way to get up and get out, but it was pointless. She was stuck right here. Trapped. This was the hand God had dealt her with, and she was going to have to fucking take it.

Because there was nothing she could do to change it.

She waited for him to hit her again. Waited for that punch. Waited for the blow that finally finished her off. But it wasn't coming. She'd been waiting a long time at this point, and she had no idea why he'd stopped. Maybe he hadn't stopped. Maybe he'd just punched her so much that she'd lost sense of what hurt and what didn't. Just like Grace, all that time ago. The burn wounds rendering it impossible to feel physical pain in certain places.

But no. She could still feel pain. He'd just... stopped.

She squinted ahead through swollen eyes and saw him standing in front of her, knife in hand. Belt on his waist laced with keys, with other smaller knives and tools of torture.

He looked at her closely. Studied her like some kind of zoo animal. Some kind of exhibit in a museum. Like he was trying to figure out what to do with her next.

"You know," he said. "Hard as it might be for you to believe, I actually don't like doing this."

And Aoife laughed. She wasn't sure which dark, demented, messed-up part of herself it came from. But she actually laughed.

"Find that funny?" Ramiro asked. "Good to know you've got a sense of humour."

"Spare me the bullshit," Aoife wheezed, free of her gag now. "I know how you people think. How you operate. I... I know what goes on in your heads. The lies you... the lies you tell yourselves. To make yourselves feel better. But you're all the same. Deep down, you're all the same."

"That sounds an awfully simplistic way of looking at things. But go on. Enlighten me. Why are we all the same, Aoife?"

Aoife coughed, spat out a tooth. Snorted up blood. "Because you're all just after one thing. Power. Power you didn't have in your lives before. Power you didn't have because you were worthless. Because you were inferior. Power you've spent your whole lives wishing you had. And now you've got your own little playground. But it's not real. None of it is real. And one day, one day, it'll all come crashing down. And when it does... when it does, you'll still be that scared little child, that meek little man, right at the centre. Before you had power."

Ramiro didn't say anything. He just stood there, knife in hand.

And then his smile widened.

He walked over to her.

"I'll show you what power is."

He lifted the knife, and she tensed up. Braced herself for it. Because this was it. This was the moment that everything had been building to. This was the moment she'd tried to fight against, tried to resist. But the moment she could resist no more.

She waited for the knife to puncture her chest or her throat when suddenly he placed it in her hand, right behind her.

And then he stepped back.

Smiled.

"Power is being able to stand here, knowing you've got a knife in your hand."

And then he stepped forward again.

Tugged at the ties around her wrists.

Hard.

And then he split them apart.

Pushed her back to the floor; now she was off the chair.

"Power is being able to look down at you while you've got a knife and know you couldn't do anything even if you wanted to."

Then suddenly, he lurched towards her. Grabbed her. Pressed his body right up to hers. Pulled the knife around and pushed it to his chest.

He stared down into her eyes, breathing that sickly sour breath all over her face.

"Power is this knife, to my chest, and knowing you can't do a thing. Because you're too weak. You're too pathetic. And because you know damn well if you did something... things would be so much worse for you. And so much worse for Billy."

Aoife's muscles seized up.

She wanted to stab him.

She wanted to kill him.

But that threat...

Ramiro smiled. He turned the knife around, and then he snatched it from Aoife's hand.

"You don't have to worry about Billy," he said. "Not as long as you comply. Not as long as you're a good little goose. And you know what? I think you will be. I really do."

He came forward again and licked her ear. Stuck his tongue deep inside it, then stepped away and licked his lips. She could see how hard he was.

"We can make you good. We can make you compliant. And when you are... Well. I think you'll be a damned good little slave."

He unclipped his belt and threw it to one side.

Went to unzip his flies.

Then, suddenly, the door to the room Aoife was trapped in opened.

"Boss," the man said. Aoife didn't recognise him.

But he was covered in blood.

And he looked terrified.

"Christopher?" Ramiro said, zipping his flies back up. "What the hell?"

"They—they attacked. They've taken it."

"Slow down, Christopher. They've taken what—"

"Polly's place!" Christopher said. "Jarrod. Jarrod..."

Ramiro seemed to stop right there. Almost like he'd been struck by lightning.

He looked back at Aoife and sighed. "I'll deal with you later."

And then he walked out of the room, slamming the door behind him, leaving Aoife lying there on the floor in the darkness, battered and bruised.

But Aoife smiled.

Because he'd left his belt here on the floor beside her.

The belt filled with blades.

CHAPTER FORTY-FOUR

"Slow down and tell me exactly what happened."

Christopher was shaking like a fucking wreck, which pissed Ramiro the hell off. He always thought Christopher was tough. Always thought he was no-nonsense. Part of why he'd sent him down to Polly's place in the first fucking place, so he could keep meatheads like Fraser in check.

But now he was back here, and he was being an emotional fucking wreck, and Ramiro could really do without that right now.

"Christopher," he said, planting his hands on his shoulders. "Slow down. Take a fucking breath. And tell me exactly what happened."

Christopher puffed his lips out. There were a lot of people around, here in the middle of the camp, staring on. Wondering what the hell this was all about. Some of them looked spooked, and that pissed Ramiro off even more. His people shouldn't get spooked. They were supposed to be tough. They were supposed to be the ones doing the fucking spooking.

Christopher had caused a goddamned scene, and he would pay for it in due course.

"I was on watch," Christopher said.

Clearly not doing a fucking good job, though, were you?

"I... I had a scrap with Fraser."

"A scrap with Fraser?"

"That—that doesn't matter. I... We had a scrap. Then something happened."

"I can see something happened," Ramiro said. "But you need to be more specific. What's all this about Jarrod?"

"He—he came. He must've... he must've heard about what happened at Polly's somehow."

"That's impossible," Ramiro said. Wasn't it? There's no way Jarrod could've found out. Unless they had a mole somewhere...

He looked around at these faces and these eyes peering back at him, and suddenly he felt mistrustful of them. Like he didn't trust a single fucking one of them.

He needed to keep his shit together. Needed to keep his cool.

Couldn't let his insecurities and paranoia get the better of him. Not now.

"Tell me what happened. As it happened."

Christopher took a breath. "He shot Fraser. And then... and then they tried to shoot at me. But I... I don't know. I think they wanted me to run."

"They wanted you to run?"

"To send a message. Or something. I don't know. But I... I couldn't stay. I couldn't. I had to run. They would've killed me. They would've killed me, and I had to come back and warn you. I —I had to come back and tell you what'd happened. I had to, Ramiro. I had to."

Ramiro felt for Christopher. He really did. He bought into his fear. And he understood why he'd come back here to warn him.

But at the same time... he was angry.

And that anger just bubbled away at the surface.

And he needed to do something about it.

"Please, Ramiro," Christopher said. "I didn't—I didn't mean

to abandon the post. I just… I needed to get back here. I needed to let you know. But I… I think I've fucked up. I think I might've… I think they might've…"

"Followed you back," Ramiro said, finishing Christopher's sentence for him. He felt resigned about it. He'd accepted it already. There was a reason they lived out here in the middle of nowhere. Their last home? Destroyed by Jarrod. Took them months to regroup and find someplace new. Ended up invading this place, well out of the way.

A place Jarrod didn't know the location of.

A place nobody knew the location of.

"You came back here," he said. "And you led them right towards us. Is that what you're trying to tell me?"

Christopher shook his head. Sobbed. "Please. I didn't mean to. I… I'm sorry."

Ramiro took a deep breath.

Sighed.

And then he smiled. "It's okay. I understand."

Christopher raised his head. Frowned. "What—"

Ramiro punched him.

Hard.

And then he jumped on top of him and punched him again.

And again.

And again.

Harder and harder. The back of his skull cracking against a rock underneath.

Harder and harder and harder as he slapped and kicked and wailed.

Harder and harder and harder until—

Crack.

His skull split open.

Hot blood covered Ramiro's fists.

He stood up. Shaking. His entire fucking body shaking. His people staring on.

"Get down to the fucking gates and make fucking sure none of them get within a mile of this place."

"I think it's already too late for that, boss."

Ramiro frowned. "What?"

Jamie, wimpy little shit, stared at the ground. "They're… they're already close. They'll be here soon. We don't have much time left."

Ramiro looked around at his people. All of them staring back at him. Fear intensifying.

"Well, what are you waiting for? Get to the gates and fucking defend them, for fuck's sake!"

He reached for his belt to grab his keys and realised he'd left it in the outhouse.

"Fuck. Fucking hell."

He walked back towards that outhouse, physically shaking. He saw the way his people looked at him. And as much as he was going to stand up, as much as he was going to be a leader, as much as he was going to *fight*… he felt afraid.

Very fucking afraid.

Because Jarrod wasn't going to mess around.

He opened the door to the outhouse, and he was so caught up in fear about what was happening that it was only at the last possible moment that he remembered he'd untied Aoife from her chair.

It was only at the last possible moment that he looked into the darkness and realised she wasn't where he'd left her.

And it was only at the last possible moment when he felt the sharp, searing pain split through his back and someone pushing him to the solid floor.

CHAPTER FORTY-FIVE

Aoife saw Ramiro's body lying in front of her, and she knew she had to act fast.

Very fucking fast.

She was sore. Her body ached all over. She could barely breathe with the clotted blood in her nostrils. She was missing teeth, and the blood kept on building up in her mouth, the taste of metal so strong, so intense.

But she was on her feet. She was alive.

And she was standing over Ramiro.

It'd all happened so fast. He'd left the room, forgetting his belt, leaving it on the floor. She'd grabbed it. Searched it quickly. Then she'd run over to the door, waited behind it. She could hear him shouting out there. Something was going down. She could hear gunfire, and she could hear people calling out. Desperate shouts and cries.

She didn't know what it was, but she knew it had to be something to do with this Jarrod.

The one who had taken Polly's camp.

She thought about that look of fear she'd seen on Ramiro's face the moment his friend, Christopher, mentioned Jarrod.

The way he'd turned pale.

And she wondered just what hold that man had over Ramiro and his people.

Then she refocused on the present. On what was right in front of her.

Ramiro lay on the floor. Stab wound in his back. Bleeding out. Totally still.

She'd stabbed him. Pushed him to the floor. Held that blade there for just a while. Waited until he gargled his last breath.

And it felt like an injustice, weirdly. Ramiro deserved a far worse, far more painful death than the one he'd got for the way he'd treated Billy. The way he'd treated so many people.

But he was down, now.

He was down, and Aoife had one job.

She had to get Billy out of here.

She had to take this one opportunity—the only opportunity she was going to get—and she had to escape.

She could worry about the details another time.

She searched Ramiro's body for keys. Then she remembered. The belt. The belt was full of keys.

The key to wherever Billy was had to be on there.

Shit.

Which key was it?

And where the hell *was* Billy?

She kept on searching that belt for the keys, stuffing them all into her pocket in her shaking hands. Some of them had numbers on. Some of them had letters on. None of it made sense.

One step at a time, Aoife. One step at a time.

She grabbed more and more of those keys, and then she stood up and made her way to the open door. She could hear more gunshots outside. More shouting, more fighting.

She went to step out when she heard footsteps running towards the door.

"Ramiro? We need you out here!"

Shit. This bloke was going to find Ramiro's body.

He was going to find him, and then he was going to kill her—and then there was no hope for Billy whatsoever.

"Boss? You in there?"

Aoife stood there. Frozen. Like the proverbial rabbit in the motherfucking headlights.

She looked at that open door.

At the growing morning light outside.

And then she ran towards that door and slammed it shut.

"Boss?" A knock on the door. "I know—I know we ain't supposed to interrupt. But we're dying out here. We need your help."

Aoife held her breath.

Held still. Totally still.

Please don't come in. Please don't fucking come in...

Another knock on the door. More frantic, this time.

"Boss, this ain't good. And I don't mean to beg. I know you don't like that. But... but we really, really need you right now."

Aoife gripped the knife to her chest.

She didn't want to have to use it again. She was shaking. She knew she was capable of fighting, more than capable of standing up for herself. But she wasn't sure she had much fight left in her.

But this man. He wasn't giving up. He wasn't going away.

He was going to come through that door. And she had to be ready. Just like she was ready with Ramiro.

She held her breath, stepped to the side of the door, and waited for him to barge inside.

But then nothing happened.

No bang on the door.

Nothing.

She held her breath. Waited. It didn't sound like that man was outside anymore. It sounded like he'd gone.

Which meant she had her moment.

She had the perfect moment to get the hell out of here, to get the fuck away.

To find Billy and then escape.

She turned and went to open the door.

Pulled it open and stepped out into the fresh air outside.

She looked around, disoriented. She was on top of a hill. It looked like the place Jon had brought her to, where he'd lost his life, where the rest of his people had fallen. There was no sign of them now.

But the man called Christopher lay on the ground before her.

He didn't look in a good way.

She looked around, over towards where the gunshots and the shouting came from. She could hear the shouting down there. There was some sort of battle going down. Some sort of conflict.

She had to turn her attention from that. Whatever was going on, it wasn't her fight.

Her fight, her priority, was finding Billy.

She looked around. Looked at the caravans. Looked at the cabin she'd been locked inside. She looked at the old cafe in the distance, covered in blacked-out windows. She had no idea where he was, where to go. It didn't look like there were many places to hide these slaves. Not here.

She went to run over there—or limp over there, rather—when she suddenly saw something over to her right.

Another little cabin. A little hut. Looked like it'd been a public toilet once upon a time.

The door was partly open.

A man peeked out.

And in front of him, right in front of him...

"Billy," Aoife muttered.

She waited until the door closed, as much as it went against her instincts. She waited until she was absolutely sure he wasn't looking. Then she ran over to that public toilet stall.

She had to get Billy out of there, but she had to be careful.

That man in there would probably shoot the second someone opened the door.

She looked up, right to the top of the toilet stall. There had to be another way in. Over her shoulder, more gunshots. More gunfire. More shouting and desperate crying.

She grabbed the top of the door. Climbed up this side of the stall. Almost fell off at the first attempt. She was so out of breath. So out of all strength. So in pain.

But she had to climb.

She had to keep trying.

She reached the roof of the toilets and fully expected fate not to be on her side once again when she noticed something.

A vent.

A vent, right above her.

Only it had been torn away.

There was a wide opening on the roof.

A way in.

She climbed over to it.

Peeked down.

Inside, she saw them both, and her stomach sank.

Billy.

Billy, and a man holding on to him.

Stroking him. Reassuring him.

"It's okay, my sweet," he said. "Don't worry, baby boy. You and me will hide in here. We'll wait this out. And then we'll get away, and we can be together, just the two of us. You don't need to worry, sugar."

Aoife knew she should keep her calm.

She knew she should maintain her composure.

But she couldn't.

She just couldn't.

She dropped down through that vent.

Landed right behind the man.

He started to turn around, but she didn't give him the chance.

She buried her knife into his throat.

Stuck it in, right deep.

Then she stabbed him again, and again, and again.

She pushed him to the floor. Kicked his twitching body.

And she stared down at him, shaking, covered in blood. Anger and that familiar old urge for vengeance taking over completely.

"Aoife?"

And then hearing his voice just calmed her.

Hearing his voice made her feel okay, made her remember why she was here, right away.

She turned to Billy, and then she grabbed him. Hugged him. Held him close. Even though she was covered in blood.

"It's okay. I've got you. You don't have to worry anymore. We're going to get out of here. I've got you."

"Never leave me again," Billy said. "Never leave me. Please."

"I won't leave you. I won't leave you ever again. I promise."

And she meant it. She wasn't just saying it for his benefit anymore. She really meant it.

She looked at him, tears rolling down her face, and she smiled.

"Let's get out of here," she said. The gunfire and explosions and shouting getting louder and louder. But seeming further and further away from her, from the pair of them. "Let's…"

"I don't think so," a voice said.

Aoife's body went numb.

Totally cold.

She looked over Billy's shoulder, and she couldn't believe what she was seeing.

Ramiro stood by the door.

Hunched over. Gripping the wound on his side.

But standing there.

Blocking their way out.

"You two aren't going anywhere."

CHAPTER FORTY-SIX

Aoife saw Ramiro standing by the door and couldn't believe her fucking luck.

He was hunched over on one side. Holding on to that bleeding wound. The morning light behind him was getting brighter now. But his silhouette was big and dark and blocking hers and Billy's way out.

She held on to Billy. Held him close. Looked up at the vent she'd just dropped through.

"Don't even think about it," Ramiro muttered. There was no happiness to his voice anymore. No confidence. No joy. "You won't get out. You won't... you won't stand a chance."

Aoife shook her head. Outside, she could hear Ramiro's people under attack. The gunshots, the explosions. It certainly sounded like they were having their asses handed to them.

"It's over, Ramiro."

Ramiro shook his head. "You don't get to decide when it's over."

"Your people are dying. You're wounded. Badly wounded. Not badly enough, in my opinion, but that's a mistake I won't make again. Step aside. Give this boy a chance to live. He's been robbed of life enough as it is. Don't make him suffer any more."

Ramiro smiled. Even though he looked wounded, down and out, there was a part of him that looked like he was still enjoying this. "Look at you. Giving your orders. And still... and still you're begging me. Pathetic. Strong, sure. Got closer to me than... than anyone has. But not strong enough."

He stumbled towards Aoife, but he was staring at Billy.

Aoife tightened her grip on the knife. "You're making a big mistake. Best thing you could do is walk away and die gracefully."

And then she saw the shaking knife in Ramiro's hand. Shaking so much, he could barely hold on to it. He didn't look as powerful or as threatening anymore.

And yet there was still an air about him that Aoife found... dangerous.

"There's only one person who can protect you now, Billy," Ramiro said. "And you know who that is."

Billy shook his head. Cried. "I'm... I don't want your protection anymore."

"What you said to me down at Polly's," Ramiro said, getting closer. "I know you didn't mean it. I know you were just afraid. I know you just missed some parts of your life how it used to be. And that's normal. It's normal, and I get it. But think about the good things, Billy. Don't let her poison you. Remember the play days we had with the other kids. Remember the football matches. I know... I know there's been some dark times. But it's not been all bad. And we can change. *I* can change. I can... I can do things differently. You just... you just have to trust me."

He stood there right in front of Billy and Aoife, shaking, wobbling on his feet. Aoife was amazed he still had the strength to stand. Especially since she didn't feel like she had much strength herself.

But the way he looked at Billy. And the way Billy looked back at him...

He held out a hand. A shaking hand.

"I know I haven't been great with you. But... but things can be better. We can leave here and... and we can start again, and we can be better. All of us can be better."

He looked at Aoife now, and she felt sick. Was he actually begging? Pleading?

He'd lost all his sense of terror. Lost all his composure.

He looked like a weak man and nothing more.

A failed leader.

He held out that shaking hand to Billy and dropped to his knees, blood trickling from his lips.

"Please, Billy. Please."

Billy stood right in front of him as he knelt there, shaking, twitching.

And then he reached out.

For a moment, Aoife thought he was going to grab his hand.

For a moment, she thought he was going to fall into his clutches again. Even though he was almost dead, it looked like Ramiro still had this hold over him.

But Billy stood tall.

He looked into his eyes, tears streaming down his face.

"I hate you," he said. "And I'll never come back. I'm... I'm glad you're all dying. I'm glad Jarrod came. And I—I hope he kills everyone here."

Ramiro's eyes narrowed. "Little shit. Just you wait til I—"

"I'm not scared of you," Billy said. "Not anymore."

He lifted his hands, and Aoife thought he might just do something violent to him. Something violent *she* wanted to do to him.

But this was Billy's moment.

And all he did?

He pushed Ramiro back.

A gentle push to the floor.

Ramiro fell back. The way out of here was clear.

He lay there on the floor, in front of the door. Tried to drag himself back up. But it was pointless. He wasn't going anywhere.

"Come on, Billy, you little weakling. After everything I did to you, and you're... you're still too scared to hurt me. Still too afraid to do anything to me."

But Billy walked past him. Didn't look at him. Not again.

"Cowards," Ramiro coughed, spluttered. "Cowards, the pair of you. You'll never make it out there. You can run all you want, but you'll never make it. Because you're mine. And... and you'll never forget the things we did to you, Billy. You'll never sleep at night knowing what we did. And what we'll do when we catch you again."

Billy stopped.

Looked back.

Went to say something.

Then took a breath and turned around.

Aoife stepped over to Ramiro. Looked down at him.

His eyes narrowed, a look of disgust on his face. "You."

"Billy might be forgiving," Aoife said. "Billy might not want to be violent. But I'm not quite as much of a pacifist."

Ramiro's eyes widened. "What—"

Aoife kicked him in the throat.

Then she buried her knife into the stab wound on his side.

Made him cry out. Made him scream.

Grabbed his mouth and covered it to muffle his cries.

"Feel this," Aoife said. "Feel it and know I was right when I told you how it was going to end."

She dug even deeper into the wound on his side.

Had her whole damned fist in there now.

And then she dug that knife in even deeper and started twisting it around his innards.

Hot blood pouring out over her hand.

Rage filling her body.

And feeling good about it.

"Aoife," Billy said.

She looked up at him. Saw sadness and fear in his wide eyes.

And she knew she'd been lost in revenge. She knew that lust for vengeance had taken her again.

She looked down at Ramiro, and she spat on his face.

"Someone else can finish you off, you trash."

She yanked the knife out of his body.

Then she stood up and walked over to Billy's side.

They stood at the door, the pair of them. Blood dripping from Aoife's hand. The sound of gunfire and explosions still so noisy.

She looked at Billy, put her clean hand on his head, and she smiled.

"Never leave me again," he said.

"I'll never leave you again."

"Promise?"

Aoife hesitated. Just for a moment, she hesitated.

The fear.

The reluctance...

Then she took a breath and let it all drift away.

"I promise."

She looked back at Ramiro as he lay there, struggling for his life.

And then she tightened her grip on Billy's hand, just a little.

"Let's get out of here," she said. "Let's..."

"You'll never get away."

That voice.

A voice she recognised.

A voice she hadn't heard for so long.

So real.

So... present.

She looked around into the darkness, beyond Ramiro, and she saw her silhouette.

"Kayleigh," Aoife said.

Kayleigh stood there. She couldn't make her out properly, but there was something different about her. Something *off* about her.

Rex by her side.

She walked towards Aoife, who was frozen to the spot.

She's not real. She's gone. None of this is real.

"You won't get away because you don't *deserve* to get away."

"Shut up."

"For what you did... you don't deserve peace."

"Shut up!"

"Aoife..."

Billy's voice. Drifting into her consciousness.

But distant. Hazy.

Like *he* was the lie, and Kayleigh and Rex here were real.

She stepped forward, and Aoife saw her more clearly.

She saw the burns all over her body.

She saw her, and she felt so guilty for leaving her behind.

"You don't deserve anything," Kayleigh said. Crying blood. Anger in her eyes. "And you won't be able to protect him. You won't be able to protect anybody. Because you always leave them behind. It's what you do."

"Aoife," Billy said. His voice barely cutting through. "Don't listen to her. She's lying. It's not true..."

She looked down at him and saw his gorgeous little face. Those trusting eyes that had seen so many horrors.

And she felt so sorry for him. Because she knew Kayleigh was right. Bad things awaited people who were attached to her.

"You can wait here," Kayleigh said, staggering closer. "You can stay here, with me and Rex. Because that's what you deserve. That's exactly what you deserve, and you know it."

And Aoife heard Kayleigh. She heard her, and deep down, she believed her.

"Stay with us," Kayleigh said. "Stay with us and let the boy go.

'Cause he's stronger without you. He's safer without you. You'll hold him back. You'll get him killed. And you know it."

She stared into Kayleigh's tearful, bloodshot eyes.

Loosened her grip on Billy's hand.

Kayleigh smiled.

Somewhere in the distance, Billy screamed. "Aoife! Watch…"

"I won't walk away from him," Aoife said. "I'll protect him. Just like I've always fought to protect everyone."

Kayleigh's face turned.

Aoife pulled back the knife.

Rammed it into her.

"No!" Kayleigh screamed. "No!"

She grew hazier. And then the Kayleigh of old started to return. The one who was her friend. The one she'd grown to love.

"Don't lose sight of what's most important," she said. "You've figured that out now. I know you have."

And then she heard a pop, and Kayleigh disappeared.

And then suddenly she was back. Snapped back into reality. She could hear shouting and gunshots outside. She could hear Billy crying beside her.

And she was holding onto someone who wasn't Kayleigh.

Ramiro.

He was on his feet.

Aoife had the knife buried right into his bleeding stomach.

She pushed him back onto the floor.

Looked down at him lying there.

And with certainty and some combination of sadness and relief, she knew Kayleigh was gone now. Rex was gone now.

She looked around at Billy.

Saw him looking back up at her with wide, curious eyes. "Are they gone now?" he asked.

Aoife took a deep breath.

Nodded.

"They're gone now."

She took Billy's hand in hers.

Looked back at Ramiro, just once.

For a second, just a split second, she swore she saw Kayleigh standing there in the shadows, screaming.

But this time, she turned around and ran away, with Billy's hand in hers.

oife looked back at Ramiro's camp and held Billy's hand.

The gunshots weren't as frequent anymore. There was a smell of burning in the air. The taste of smoke. And it reminded her of that day she'd turned around and looked back at Sanctuary. Watched the smoke rise, knowing full well what she was responsible for.

The death of power.

And the death of her friend.

Her best friend.

But she felt different about it, now. That moment, back in Ramiro's camp. Burying the knife into her vision of Kayleigh. Telling her that she *was* going to stand by Billy. And that she *was* going to protect him, no matter what it took.

She wasn't going to let her fear of what had happened in her past deter her.

She wasn't going to leave Billy.

She was going to fight for him.

Just like she always fought.

"Where do we go now?" Billy asked.

Aoife looked down at him. Pale. Big blue bags under his eyes. He looked exhausted like he needed a real good rest.

They both needed a real good rest, that was for sure. She'd been battered and ached like mad. Couldn't get the taste of blood out of her mouth. That rest would be a real luxury right now.

But they weren't going to get it.

Not just yet.

Aoife turned away from Ramiro's camp. She didn't know what was happening there. She didn't care, quite frankly. This Jarrod, whoever he was, had moved in by the looks of things. Replaced Ramiro and his people.

And that's how the cycle would always go. It didn't really matter who Jarrod was or who Ramiro was, or who the next goon was.

There would always be someone badder, nastier, and more powerful waiting to replace you.

And that wasn't a world Aoife wanted to participate in. Not anymore.

She took a deep breath of the cool winter air. Although, saying that... it felt warmer, somehow. Like spring air. Maybe winter was finally coming to a close, and spring was rearing its head. About fucking time.

She wanted to answer Billy's question. She wanted to tell him she had a plan. An exact plan for where she was going to take him. An exact plan for where things were going to go next.

But you know what?

She didn't see the point in lying. To herself, or Billy.

"I... I don't know where we're going now," Aoife said. "That's my honest answer."

She glanced at Billy. Half-expected him to look back at her with disappointment.

But instead, he looked... well, remarkably chilled. Remarkably content.

He actually looked *happy*.

"That's okay," he said.

Aoife smiled at him. Put a hand on his back. Allowed herself to feel his warmth, just for a second.

"I hope you're real," she said.

Billy frowned. "What?"

She shook her head. She knew it was a stupid thing to say. But she was in a goddamned honest mood, so she wasn't going to hold back anymore. "Sometimes... sometimes I think about how much I convinced myself Kayleigh and Rex were still around. How real they felt to me. Because I was lonely. And I... I dunno. Sometimes I just wonder if you're real. Or whether you're just something my mind sent me to get through what I was dealing with."

She felt stupid. Her cheeks flushed. Who the fuck was the adult, and who was the child, now?

But when she looked back at Billy, she saw he was smiling wider.

"Does it matter?" he asked.

She smiled back at him. Laughed. "It's a fair point."

He squeezed her hand. Tighter still. "I'm real, though. Sometimes I think the same about you."

"Oh yeah?"

Billy nodded. "I sometimes think I'm back there. The horrible things happening to me. And then I think of adventures I'd go on. I think about running away. I... I disappear there sometimes. Maybe I just... maybe I just haven't got back yet. Or woke up."

Aoife ruffled his hair. "Look at us. A pair of lunatics who don't even know if each other is real."

"Good company," Billy said.

"Yeah," Aoife said. "The best."

They stood there a little while. She had no idea how long. But it was nice, just standing here with him. Standing here without any worries. Standing here and pretending nothing else mattered in the world.

Because right now, even if just for a moment, nothing else really did matter.

She heard shouting behind her. Sounded like voices getting closer. And a surge of adrenaline crept up her spine. A reminder. A reminder that they weren't safe. A reminder that they were *never* safe.

But as long as they were together... things were going to be okay.

Things were going to work out.

She looked at Billy.

He looked back at her.

Both of them smiled.

"Come on," Aoife said. "Let's get going."

And then together, the pair of them ran away from Ramiro's place, ran through the trees, and ran towards whatever future awaited them.

Together.

CHAPTER FORTY-EIGHT

She walked through the tall, frozen grass, wooden stick in hand, and saw the place she'd been looking for right up ahead.

She'd been walking a long time. Felt like forever. But then so did everything these days. Kind of how it went when you were a cripple like she was.

She remembered the flames.

Remembered just how hot the smoke was, so thick in her lungs, like tar.

She remembered that moment, on the verge of blacking out, where she was convinced it was over. Convinced it was the end.

And then she remembered waking up.

Dragging herself towards that ladder.

Clambering her way out, towards the light...

She shook her head. She didn't want to think about the rest.

She looked down at the place she'd been heading for. The place she'd been searching for, for so long.

Looked at the tall walls. At the metal gates.

And at just how like Sanctuary it looked.

She took a deep breath of that cold air, and she heard panting beside her.

She looked down.

Saw the dog beside her, wagging his docked little tail.

And she smiled at him. Never had been a big dog lover. But she'd sure as hell warmed to this one.

It was nice to have a friend in this world.

"Come on," she said. "Let's go check it out."

She took a deep breath, and she walked towards the Scottish district, praying for a miracle.

And as Kayleigh walked, she couldn't help but hope—and pray—that by the force of some divine intervention, Aoife would be right here waiting for her.

* * *

END OF BOOK 7

Battle the Darkness, the eighth book in the Survive the Darkness series, is now available.

If you want to be notified when Ryan Casey's next novel is released—and receive an exclusive post apocalyptic novel totally free—sign up for the author newsletter: ryancaseybooks.com/fanclub